LUCID DREAMS

JOHN LOCATELLI

PEANUT BUTTER
PUBLISHING

Seattle, Washington
Portland, Oregon
Denver, Colorado
Vancouver, B.C.

Manufactured in the United States of America.
Cover Design by David Marty Design

Published by Peanut Butter Publishing
226 Second Ave. West
Seattle, WA 98119

LCCCN: 97-65741
ISBN: 0-89716-711-2
A1.0047

For my wife Helen,
and our children
Amy, Mary, Adam and Megan

TABLE OF CONTENTS

CHAPTER 1

FEEDING TIME

THE JAWS OPENED ever so slightly. He had meant to use his left hand this time, but he forgot. So what? Did it make any difference which hand he used? Sunday was his left hand, Monday his right, Tuesday—well, he couldn't remember; besides there had been so many days. Lots of days, lots of money. How much money he didn't know; he didn't care to know.

He never liked to know how much money he had. When he was a child and played Monopoly, he never counted his money. He let it pile up, hidden under the game board. Not counting it made the pile seem bigger; not knowing was exciting. At the end of the game, counting the money was like finding buried treasure. When the game board was finally lifted up, then, only then, was the vastness of the treasure known. He was always surprised at how much he had secretly hidden, even from himself. Many years later he was still the same little boy, still hiding treasure. But soon, very soon, he would pry open the box, and then the alligator would have to feed itself.

The jaws opened slightly more. Was he becoming too confident? A mistake, a miscalculation here would be nasty. He'd done this so

I

many times he'd gotten bored and lax. So lax that he barely paid attention anymore.

Was he seven or eight? Seven it must have been. Yes, seven. That was when he figured out what happened when he learned something new. At the start he knew he was careful and cautious, but he also knew he learned quickly. Then he knew he excelled. It was boredom that came next, rapidly replaced by overconfidence. He didn't like to think about the final stage: it was always the same. Understanding the course of events couldn't prevent the events from reaching the final outcome. At eight it was only his bike crashing into a wall. At twelve it was only a few stitches. At twenty-five the tip of a finger. Now at forty he was getting dangerously close to the final stage again, way too close. Part of a finger was OK, but to become overconfident now would be deadly.

In a moment the jaws would be open just enough. Timing was everything, but somehow he knew he couldn't look this time either, he had to do the rest by feel and sound.

The first accident he ever remembered seeing was one he made the mistake of looking at. He couldn't forget the images of the wreck. So he taught himself not to look, and it had proven to be good training. Now he had no images to think about, nothing to keep him awake at night. Besides, depending on feel and sound made him concentrate and maybe, just maybe, would keep him from reaching overconfidence, and disaster.

The jaws snapped shut. Then he heard the splash. The splash meant it was over for him. How long for the other man? He didn't know, and he didn't want to think about it. Several minutes, he supposed. He read that a man caught by surprise was too shocked to feel any pain. This thought made him feel better; this thought was what he wanted to believe.

He looked at the famous picture on the wall of the soldier, back arched, arms flung out above his head, caught at the moment of death. He saw beauty in death. No artist, he thought, could have drawn a more graceful arch, sketched a more dramatic line. As a boy he liked to watch pods split and spill their seeds to the earth. There too, he thought, the pods were arched as they gave birth to new life. He studied that unknown man at the instant of death. He saw in the arched back and the outstretched arms a body spilling forth its reborn life, a body spilling forth its soul into the eternal. In death is beauty, he mused, and now he was creating beauty at the death of another unknown man. The rhythm of the jaws, the graceful movement of his hands with their graceful, slender fingers, the perfect timing, the final closing of the jaws, and the moment when the soul was cast from its human pod. All these thoughts were a comfort to him.

The noise of the jaws closing reminded him of another sound from his childhood. It was a sound he didn't like and didn't want to remember. He hated waiting in line at the confessional. The church was always cold and empty, except for the few people waiting in line and the few saying penance in the pews. All he had to do was to go in, carefully close the door, kneel on the cold stone, and wait for the priest to open the door that covered the window draped with purple velvet. The snapping open of that door was the sound he wished he could forget. He was frightened of having to confess his sins in front of the priest, but even more frightened of having no sins to confess. Better to play safe with made up sins and hide what shouldn't be spoken. So when he had no sins he hurriedly made some up. Fighting with a brother was an old standby, and was good for only a few Hail Mary's. He wouldn't want to have to confess to a priest now; what made-up sin could possibly hide what he now did? Besides, the alligator was hungry, not him. It would happen to them anyway, and this way it was quick.... His

3

thoughts were suddenly ended by the sound of a boat whistle. Other thoughts raced through his mind and words spilled out. "What's a sailboat doing here so early in the morning? Lucky this wasn't a few minutes earlier!" Then, as it had many times before, the whistle called him back to his work. A day that started with beauty and death would end normally, as days end for countless others.

CHAPTER TWO

JOB 1:7

"**A**ND THE LORD said unto Satan, 'Whence come thou?' Then Satan answered the Lord, and said, 'From going to and fro in the earth, and from walking up and down in it.' Job 1:7," Stephen recited from memory.

What have I gotten myself into? thought Karen. I've taken a part-time position as a data analyst, and the man I'm supposed to be working for is quoting the Bible to me? Maybe I should quit before he goes any further. These middle-aged men are all alike. First they quote the Bible or their mothers. Next it's Dr. Ruth. Then they are telling you the same tired lines, the same tired promises, the cock and bull stories of how sensitive they have become. Ick! They make my flesh crawl! Sure mister, yeah I know, you might not have the energy of someone my age, but you know how to satisfy a woman from years of experience. Sure mister, but not with me!

Karen looked at Stephen with what she hoped was a proper show of interest and asked, "What about the Devil? I mean, what's he got to do with my job?"

"Karen, do you know the only thing that can stop the Devil from striding back and forth across the earth?" Stephen asked.

"Not really," replied Karen, valiantly trying to maintain a look of interest .

"Come on, what can stop the Devil, what's the principle involved here?" Stephen asked, looking directly into her eyes.

Karen didn't want to return the look. He was an ordinary man, not particularly handsome except for his eyes. His eyes always seemed to be asking for more than what was said. It was as if his eyes had their own thoughts and were waiting for an answer only they knew was yet to come. So, she avoided his eyes and looked around his office instead. What a total mess, she said to herself. He's piled books on top of old journal articles, on top of phone books and old catalogues. Is that a heap of old newspapers under his desk? I wonder if those are homemade shelves over his head. Papers are hanging off them like moss. How disgusting! Archeologists would love this room. They could spend years peeling back the various layers, reconstructing his life.

"Karen!" Stephen interrupted her thoughts. "What about the Devil?"

This time Karen looked at his eyes. Karen liked men to look at her eyes when they spoke to her, but not this man. She wished he would look away, but he kept looking and now she felt she had to answer something. "Well," Karen said. "Are you looking for the principle behind the question? Then it must be something or someone as powerful or more powerful than the Devil."

"Yes, yes," he interjected. "That's the principle! In order to stop a powerful force an even more powerful force is needed. In this case, that force is God!"

So what? thought Karen, but managed to look interested.

"Now take large air masses," Stephen continued, warming even more to his subject. "They stride across the earth like the Devil described in Job. The earth is their domain. They cross the oceans

and continents with ease. Warm moist air from the equator moving northward, frigid air from the poles plunging toward the
equator. Huge storms are spawned where they collide. What do
you think can stop these masses of air that think they own the
earth?"

Karen shifted slightly in her chair, but didn't reply to Stephen's
question. Those eyes, she thought, are downright spooky. And this
conversation is getting a bit strange.

"From Job we learned the force must be more powerful than
the air masses themselves," Stephen continued. "Of course. It has
to be the very earth itself, the mountains and the valleys. Only
these can turn the air masses from their path."

"What's that got to do with the work I will be doing for you?"
Karen asked, paying closer attention as she found herself becoming more interested in what Stephen was saying.

Stephen leaned back in his chair, glancing out the door as if to
see if anyone else might be coming by, and then answered Karen.
"For this project I'm mostly interested in one air mass and one
mountain range. Are you familiar with the geography of North
Carolina?"

Karen nodded.

"Good. Then you know the Appalachian Mountains are parallel
to the coast, but are inland several hundred miles. Between the
mountains and the coast are low hills that abut the flat coastal
plain. Under the right conditions cold air moves onshore, flowing
inland, but nothing can stop it, that is until it tries to breast the
Appalachians. Meeting its match in the mountains and not being
able to move further westward, the cold air is forced to flow south-
ward covering the land in a cold blanket between the mountains
and the coast. Two titans clash, the winner yields not an inch, the
vanquished retreats to the south. God and the Devil locked in bat-

tle, but was it God who won or the Devil? Do you have time to listen to the rest?" Stephen asked as he again looked into the hallway.

"Sure," replied Karen, glancing into the hallway herself.

"Good! Now, if warm air tries to move inland, being lighter it moves up over the cold air forming a weather front between the warm and cold air. This causes all kinds of interesting and unique weather. However, there will be lots of time to learn the details later. Now we have to start you on your work."

Stephen leaned forward, making his points with his finger on the desk. "First, you will need to look over Jim Fulton's files on the computer, clean out all the useless ones, and rename others you want to keep so you can remember what they are. Does it seem a little cold in here?" Not giving Karen time to answer, Stephen quickly said, "Why don't you close the door, and that will keep the draft out."

Karen hadn't noticed a draft, but turned to close the door. While her back was turned she thought she heard the sound of papers moving, but when she turned to face Stephen again, she couldn't see what, if anything, had been moved.

"You will want to keep most of the programs and most of the data files, but each one will have to be checked, one by one," he continued. "It used to be that when a student left, most of the stacks of paper left behind were garbage. Now it's stacks of computer files, hidden behind names forgotten even by the author. I'd like to tell you to just delete them all and not waste your time looking at each of them, but I can't. There isn't much use in redoing his work if it already exists in a file, but some work might have to be redone if you can't figure out how he named or stored his files."

"Did Fulton leave without cleaning out his files?" asked Karen, noticing that Stephen seemed more relaxed now that the door had been closed.

"Yes, and what a mess that created. He just never showed up for work one day. That wasn't unusual for Jim as he used to work his own hours. After a few days, the secretary called his apartment, but she couldn't reach him. The police finally had the landlord open the door."

"What was there?" Karen directed her attention right at Stephen.

"Nothing really. The funny thing was he had apparently walked out one day, taking only some clothes and his suitcase. We haven't heard from him, and to tell you the truth, I really don't care, except it will delay my research having to start you cold on the project. The police didn't find any reason to continue the investigation, except to keep him on the missing persons list. So, that's about it."

"That's it?" Karen asked, becoming slightly irritated. "Some guy disappears, and so what? You seem so casual about it." She didn't say it, but Karen was thinking that he was more upset that his research would fall behind, than that a student was missing.

"Well, you have to understand," Stephen replied, sensing the irritation in Karen's voice, "that students do this all the time. I once had a student who was missing the same way. Turned out, after I spent lots of time looking for him, he showed up at my office with robes and some religious message. The excuses run the gamut — the work is too hard, or they really didn't want to be college students, or there is a problem with their love life, or almost anything. Jim will be like all the rest. Someday he will come back, collect his personal items we saved, then throw them in the nearest trash can as he leaves. Don't worry about it, OK?"

Swell, Karen said to herself. This guy will be telling the next person who works on this project not to worry that I'm missing, that he's glad I left. He probably killed him so he could hire someone else, Karen laughed to herself. The body could be in this room for years and never be found.

Still laughing inside, but only giving Stephen a slight smile, Karen said, "Sure, no problem, I'll start work on the files tomorrow. You're right. Students are like that, disappearing all the time."

"Good. Stop at the secretary's office, complete the necessary paperwork, and talk to our head programmer. He'll fix it so you can break into Jim's files and set you up with your own password. Start right down the hall in room 210. Well then, that's it until tomorrow. Oh, you can leave the door open. I don't think the draft will be a problem now that the hall has warmed up."

Karen walked towards room 210. "Room 208, room 209, room 210," Karen read in a low voice, "and I don't think the hall's any warmer." Seeing a neatly dressed woman seated behind a tidy desk, Karen said, "Hi, I'm Karen, Professor Stephen Lang's new assistant. I'm taking over from Jim Fulton."

"Hello, I'm Janet. Nice to have another woman on the floor. If God stopped making men tomorrow, that'd be fine with me. He could even make that retroactive a few years." She said with a slight smile. "Take this form, fill it out. If you have any questions when you're finished, ask away."

"Thanks," Karen replied, noticing the stark contrast between Stephen's and Janet's room. Janet had everything arranged in neat stacks. There was a place for each item, even a special holder for several newly sharpened pencils. An occasional plant broke the order, but this gave the room a homey feel.

When she finished the form, Karen, with a smile, handed it back to Janet. "Have you worked here long?" quizzed Karen.

"Lots of years," Janet answered, returning Karen's smile, "more than I care to count."

"You said I could ask any questions I wanted, so—I was wondering if I could find out some things about Stephen? It's not because I'm snoopy or anything like that, but I like to know a little about the people I work for. It helps me work better with them."

"Doesn't matter, I understand," Janet replied. "He comes across as a little different, doesn't he?"

"That's a good way of putting it."

"It's his eyes—you know—the way he looks at you. If you ever have anything to hide from him, don't look him in the eyes. You'll tell him for sure. He's brilliant, in a common sense sort of way. He could have been anything, and top at it, but like I say, he's different than most professors around here. He could have been top here too, but didn't care to."

"Why's that?" Karen broke in.

"Stephen believes that too many professors put their whole life into their work and neglect their family and friends. One day they realize what is really important in life, but then it is often times too late. They die, and that's it. Stephen gives the university the best he has when he's here, but don't even dare to intrude on his private life. Stephen doesn't give one fig whether he is famous or not. He's satisfied with who he is, and I suppose he doesn't need the OK from others. He'll be fair to you, and you might even begin to like him. Goodness, I sound like a commercial for Stephen. As you can tell, I've come to like him quite a bit over the years, and his kids too."

"He's married?" exclaimed Karen, looking surprised.

"They never married. She had some sort of an accident, never did find her body. Some people say that she just walked off one day, and never came back. That was before I came here, so I'm not sure of the correct story. He was left to raise a couple of little kids, a boy named Andy, and a girl named Jill. I think Andy was two and

Jill was eight, or close to it. Now Andy is twelve and Jill is sixteen, or Andy is eight, or something like that. Whatever their ages, they are awfully nice kids, so Stephen must have done something right. They have the cleanest language of any kids I know; kind and polite too. You don't find those qualities in many kids today. They live out in the country in a large log house he built himself. Some say he did it just to get his mind off his wife's disappearance. Looking at him a person wouldn't think he could single-handedly raise two kids and build a house, but he did. From what I've seen when he brings his kids into work, they almost worship him. Am I boring you?"

"Not at all," Karen remarked. "Not at all." Then she added, "Are you sure this is the same Stephen who has an office down the hall?"

Janet looked at Karen with renewed interest and said, "Give it some time, you might surprise yourself and actually like working for him."

Not replying to Janet's last remark, Karen started to pick up her things and turn toward the door. "Thanks for the information," she said. "Am I all done?"

"Not quite yet. Next you will have to see our computer expert. Sit down. I think you might also want to know about him. When I was young, some people became fascinated with electronics. You know, radios and such. Some of them were real strange, they couldn't talk about anything else. They took jobs in electronics, went home at night and tinkered with all sorts of radio junk. I knew a guy who had parts for everything—old TV's, radios, stereos, junk even piled on his couch. The funny thing was he never built anything that worked. Back then, it seemed mostly men became that way with electronics. Today the same thing seems to be happening with men and computers. Our computer expert, Gary, works here nine or ten hours a day, and works all night stirring around computer bits, but never biting."

Karen looked puzzled. "What do you mean, never biting?" she asked.

"Oh, it's just a joke, and a poor one, but I'm serious too," Janet said. "Only someone strange can work day and night on the same thing! Room 211, and good luck!"

Karen tried to put her thoughts in order concerning Stephen, but it was impossible at the moment. Crossing the hall toward room 211, Karen saw a rather skinny man sitting at a small desk, his face pushed close to a computer screen, typing furiously at the keyboard. Not looking up at Karen he motioned for her to sit down. Still typing at the same fast speed he said, "You're Karen, and I need to set you up with an account on the computer. You can pick your own password for security, however, I can access anyone's files, so don't keep anything you don't want me to see." Still pounding away, he continued, "One student was having an affair with a student at another university. They used the computer to send letters back and forth. They would have been better off to have used the mail since he left all the letters in his files. It made some good late night reading for me, if you catch my drift."

"I sure do," said Karen, thinking this is one guy she needed to be nice to.

It only took Gary a few minutes to set up her account, and transfer all of Jim's files to her control. "Now," he said, looking right at her for the first time, and not at the computer screen, "this is the moment at which most people stop thinking. All I ask them to do is think of a password and type it in. I type their name, look away, and they are supposed to type their password. Don't ask me why, but they just sit there frozen, wasting my time. If you can't think of one why don't we finish this tomorrow?"

"Type away," responded Karen, pointing at the keyboard. To Gary's surprise, Karen quickly typed in four letters in rapid order.

When she had gone, Gary looked her password up in his master file. There were four letters all right, and they spelled HELP.

CHAPTER THREE

BAD TIMING

WHAT A BEAUTIFUL DAY, Karen sighed to herself as she headed toward campus. Cool summer mornings are my favorite. Then again, fall mornings are my favorite as well, and I like spring mornings, too, she continued. Come to think of it, she thought with a smile, most winter mornings aren't that bad either. Crossing the last city sidewalk and stepping onto the campus was for Karen like passing into another time. The old ivy-covered buildings with their strong stone walls and leering gargoyles, the brick paths, the quiet glens, the graceful fountains, the well-tended flower beds all seemed so beautiful and so unlike the city streets Karen had just left. Karen liked to pretend that all this had been built by a people long vanished who had time for quiet thoughts, and who had left it for people like her who still found time for quiet thoughts in their busy day. The path Karen was on disappeared into a grove of tall fir trees, low level vine maple, and ferns. In a few steps the path widened into a small clearing with stone benches on either side. Sitting down on a bench, Karen thought about how much she liked this little grove and the small clearing hidden within it. The trees here seemed to hold the dampness left over from the night, and

15

the air was full of the smell of fir needles and rich earth. Glancing at the opposite bench, Karen wondered how many lovers used that bench and the hidden clearing for their own private moments.

"Oh, how I wish the earth would take me for her mistress and press me into her rich musty soil," Karen whispered. "Later when people ask me why they smell a good smell when I come close, a smell like the forest in the morning, I'll reply, 'It's because the earth is my lover—she likes to take me in the morning and leave her scent on me so I'll remember who my lover is and remain true to her.'" Karen shuddered as she thought about the smell left from some of her other lovers. It was a smell of after shave and hurried sweaty bodies, of indifference and loneliness. Karen wondered how she could be so close physically to another, but, at the very moment of intimacy, be so lonely. "Oh, if I only could carry the smell of the earth, and be her mistress," Karen sighed to herself as she rose from the bench and passed into the morning sunshine.

Karen liked the feel of the morning sun. It was soft and delicate on her face, not bold and hot as the midday sun, and not as golden and warm as the evening sun. The morning sun brought out the details of everything it touched. On Karen, it made even the finest features apparent and comely, and brought her often-hidden beauty into view. Mornings were for delicate, beautiful thoughts, for thoughts that satisfied her need to embrace all that was good in life. As she walked her thoughts turned to the midday sun. It was not as subtle. Its boldness illuminated everything, drawing the beautiful and the ugly with the same harsh strokes. I'll save midday for bold thoughts, she mused, for thoughts that face the truth, for thoughts that are not afraid to bear the reality of life. But when the evening sun casts a golden glow on everything, like a final blessing from the sun itself on the earth before nightfall, I'll stop thinking bold thoughts. I'll save evening for thoughts that reflect on the day, that recount the day's events, that affirm and bless the day.

The path took a short turn to the right and entered into Karen's favorite part of the campus. The medicinal garden was left over from another time. Once it held plants used in the treatment of many illnesses; now many of the beds were unkempt, only a few plants were cultivated for research purposes. Each bed was separated from its neighbor by gravel paths. Some beds still had the original metal plates, now faded, that held the name of the plant. Karen liked to read these faded names. "Larkspur, anise, cloves," she read out loud. How many of the plants were common, but were once important as sources of drugs? Karen thought. Moving past the last beds, Karen descended several stone stairs, passed between two ancient ornamental spruce trees, and stepped onto the green grass of a small hedge-enclosed garden. At one end stood two wooden monkeys flanking the far entrance, almost hidden by undergrowth. Across from the monkeys was a pond edged with bricks. Water was allowed to overflow the edge of the pond and trickle down a small stream which gradually disappeared into the ground, ending in a marshy area. This created a variety of growing conditions for plants whose use had long been forgotten. In the marsh, tiny plants with round green leaves and small violet flowers grew in patches alongside clumps of grass.

Karen turned towards the monkeys, nodded to them and said, "Good morning sirs, are you enjoying this beautiful garden? Am I the first visitor today? Will I be the only one to come? My smell? It's the rich morning smell of the earth. She's my lover you know. So nice of you to notice."

Sitting at the edge of the pond, Karen looked at the lilies floating silently on top of the water, and then beneath them into the clear, still water. Several fish darted from the cover of one lily pad to another. Noticing that one fish had stopped in the open, Karen slowly moved her hand just above the surface of the water, stopping over the fish. As her fingers dipped into the cool of the water, the fish disappeared into the shadows. Karen brought her hand up and watched as the water dripped back into the pond. The circles moving away from the drops rippled the lily pads and bounced off the brick edges, creating a crisscross of shadows on the bottom of the pond. "Will all my lovers be as fleeting as the ripples on this pond?" Karen asked out loud. "Will they dart into the shadows when I reach for them like these tiny fish?" Raising her hand, Karen let the last remaining drops fall onto her forehead. Turning back toward the monkeys she asked, "What is the given name of this woman about to be baptized? Who will step forward as her godparents? You will? Thank you." She turned to look at her reflection in the pond and intoned, "I baptize Karen with the very water that nourishes her lover, and charge the sun and wind to ensure she is brought up in the ways of nature." As she watched her reflection, the ringing of the chimes marking eight o'clock broke the spell. Karen hurriedly gathered her things and, rushing between the monkeys, ran towards work. I shouldn't be late for work in my second week, she worried.

Stephen slowly rose from the back seat of the bus, and gradually made his way down the aisle, carefully holding on to the metal bars overhead. He descended the stairs one step at a time, keeping a firm grip on the railing. "I could run down these steps with my eyes closed," he muttered under his breath, "but if I fall, people will shake their heads and make some remark about a rickety old man who couldn't keep his balance. If people see a little gray hair, right away they blame every mistake on age!" Stephen walked wearily onto campus. He'd seen the same brick buildings and paths, the same gargoyles staring down at him so often that he scarcely paid any attention. The bus ride was never much fun, but this morning it was worse than usual. Part way along the route the bus heater had quit working which caused the windows to steam up, and the back door leaked cold air in onto Stephen's legs. On days like this one, the worst seat on the bus was directly behind the back door; the seat Stephen was forced to take because the bus was full when it reached his stop.

Stephen turned to take his usual shortcut through the old physics building. He reached out and gripped the solid brass handles of the main doors, worn smooth from the hands of many students. Pausing for a moment, he let his fingers feel the cold smoothness of the handles. Some people, he mused, thought they could take the strength from their enemies by eating their hearts. In the future, will people be able to take the strength from the myriad that touched this handle by simply touching it?

As the door swung open he glanced at the greenish-yellow walls. "Prison walls, hospital walls, old university walls—all painted the same," he said out loud to no one in particular. "Some salesman in the twenties must have visited all the universities, hospitals, and prisons in this city, and sold all the building managers the same ugly color of paint. If there truly is a hell, I hope that salesman is roasting in it!" The smell in the building was almost as unpleasant to Stephen as the color of the walls. It brought back memories of burdensome homework assignments, boring lectures, and nervous times of waiting in the hallways before exams. The combination of stale chalk dust, old paint, and chipped plaster was almost overpowering. "Pulled down, yes these old buildings should be pulled down along with the unpleasant memories within them." Turning the corner he passed into the newer smells and more pleasant memories of his own building. The elevator was waiting with the door open, so he stepped inside and turned to push his floor number.

LUCID DREAMS

Karen bounded up the steps of the building she worked in. Swinging open the front door, she saw the elevator door just beginning to close. With one quick jump she slid between the doors. As she landed on the floor, however, she felt the elevator give a short jerk, then fall a few feet. Whirling around, Karen's frightened eyes fell upon Stephen.

"Bad timing!" Karen exclaimed.

CHAPTER FOUR

STORY TIME

"**D**IDN'T JANET WARN YOU about jumping onto this elevator?" Stephen scolded. "Now we might be here several hours until the repairman can free the safety brake and restore operation."

"I... I didn't know," Karen stammered. "She didn't tell me! Besides," Karen shot back, now starting to recover from her initial fright, "you had no business hiding in the corner of the elevator!"

Hoping to steer the conversation away from the confrontational tone it was taking, and ignoring Karen's remark, Stephen said, "This is both a freight and a passenger elevator. It was probably a mistake to allow for one elevator in a building that really needs both kinds. This isn't the first time this has happened, and it won't be the last, that is as long as we continue to hire energetic helpers. Now, tell me about your work so far," Stephen said in a normal tone, as if he carried on conversations in jammed elevators everyday. "Have you made any progress in unraveling Jim Fulton's files?"

Caught off guard by the change in Stephen's tone, Karen tried to sound business-like herself. She moved slightly out from the corner she had retreated into. "Well, Gary helped me gain access to all of

Fulton's files. There were the usual bookkeeping files, the files containing the programs needed to analyze the data, and the data files themselves. Data files were divided into both the raw data and the processed data."

"What's in the raw data files?" asked Stephen, mostly to appear interested as he was already well acquainted with the data.

"The original station reports," Karen replied, a bit surprised by his apparent lack of knowledge. "At each hour, all over the world, observers record the temperature, wind direction, and other important information. These get sent over a special circuit to universities, government offices, National Weather Service offices, and virtually anyone who can afford a computer connection. This raw data is just a series of numbers. Jim Fulton wrote several programs which decode this series into meaningful numbers and words. Another program he wrote plots the information so it can be hand-analyzed. Those station reports that were sent but couldn't be decoded were automatically put into a separate file. The idea was that these undecodable reports could be hand checked and parts of them possibly plotted. Sometimes they can be unscrambled and useful information retrieved." Karen suddenly felt a little embarrassed, as she realized that Stephen must already know all these details.

"Were those the only files you found?" Stephen asked, ignoring Karen's reddening face.

"Almost. Gary found three files that he called hidden files. Evidently it's possible to have files that don't show up on any list, but can be retrieved if one knows the right method. He was suspicious since the main storage disk had large areas that were used up, but didn't show any files. I don't understand how all this works, but Gary was able to finally isolate the files and retrieve them so we could look them over."

Stephen leaned against the wall opposite Karen. He found himself becoming more interested in what Karen was saying. "I suppose he tapped into the erotic pictures that get sent over the international network," Stephen suggested. "That would explain the large space used on the disk. I understand such things are popular with some students. The larger file might contain short movies, each about several minutes long, that can run on a personal computer."

"That's right, at least for the one file," Karen interjected, at the same time wondering how Stephen knew so much about the movies, especially since Gary told her the movies were very new, and hardly anyone was familiar with them. "The second file contained a list of scrambled reports from only one station. Fulton singled them out, I suppose, because they all had the same station name. The funny thing is, the station name doesn't appear in any station list we have, so the station name must have been transmitted with some letters in error. However, the station name always was the same sequence of letters, so some consistent error must have been happening."

"Why would Fulton want to keep such a file hidden?" Stephen asked.

"I don't know," Karen replied, shifting her weight off of her right leg which was starting to cramp up, and leaning back against the wall herself. "Gary and I can't understand why, if a consistent error was made in transmitting the station name, the station report, which immediately followed in transmission, was always scrambled in some random way. Maybe that's why he pulled them into a separate file."

"Maybe he didn't want anyone to know that he was working on something that wasn't really part of his job here," Stephen suggested. "I guess I wouldn't have liked it if I had found out that he was wasting his time on a few reports that couldn't even have been plotted anyway since the station name was unknown."

"Who knows?" Karen shrugged. "He did spend some time on those files. The third file contained a copy of a letter he sent to the main Weather Bureau Office asking about the mystery station, but he never received a reply, at least we couldn't find one. He sent the letter over the network to the Bureau addressed to all users there, so many people would have received it on their terminals. It's possible that he received a reply through the regular mail, so no record would be on the computer."

Stephen shifted his weight onto his other leg in order to ease the pain starting to throb in his back from standing so long. Middle age, thought Stephen, is definitely no fun!

"Is something wrong?" asked Karen, noticing the slight tightening of the muscles around his eyes as he shifted his stance.

"Those files, get rid of them! They aren't needed for our research, but I wouldn't be surprised if Gary wants to keep the pornography. He'll have to copy that over to his personal computer. The other two? I don't see any reason to keep them and tie up valuable disk space. Yes, better get rid of them!"

"I'd like to keep them for awhile," Karen replied. "I'm curious why Fulton singled them out, and then hid them. I'm half thinking all this is tied in with his disappearance."

"Disappearance! There wasn't any disappearance!" Stephen broke in. "I told you — a student gets fed up with school, or a girlfriend, or both, and he gets out. That's all, period. No mystery! Save space, delete the files!"

"OK," said Karen, trying not to show the frustration in her voice. "If we ever get out of this elevator, I'll talk to Gary about it."

"Good. Do you mind if I sit for awhile?" Not waiting for a reply Stephen slowly moved into the corner opposite Karen, resting his back against the wall as he sat down. "Let's not talk about work anymore. There are better ways to pass the time."

Karen shrunk deeper into the corner she was leaning against, becoming uncomfortable with the way the conversation was going. I wondered when he would get around to this, Karen thought. I can read these middle-aged men like a book. "Oh—what might that be?" she asked aloud, trying to sound uninterested.

"Story time," replied Stephen. "Let's tell stories."

"What do you mean, tell stories?" Karen asked, caught off guard by his answer. "What kind of stories?"

"You know," Stephen laughed, "a person moves his mouth and words come out. Other people listen. The words go together to make a story, a story that is interesting to the people listening. They take turns—it's fun!"

I'm not stupid, thought Karen. I know what telling a story is, but what's he leading up to?

"Well—why don't you go first, since you're the guest, so to speak," Stephen offered. "If you can't think of one, try telling one from your childhood. You had one, didn't you?"

As Karen stood thinking, Stephen looked at her with his deep, probing eyes. Stephen had met many women in his lifetime, and Karen was more ordinary looking than most of them. Her height was average and her hair, light brown in color, was cut short above her ears. Her face was pleasant enough to look at, and when she smiled she was actually pretty. Karen wasn't overweight particularly, but she was heavier than most modern women wanted to be. All these rather ordinary features, somehow combined together, made Karen attractive to him. What had his mother called women like this? he mused.

Karen, feeling Stephen staring at her, shifted uneasily in her corner. I will never get used to those eyes, she thought, becoming increasingly uncomfortable with her predicament. Stephen, noticing her discomfort, offered an apology. "I didn't mean to stare, but it is something I do because I want to get a clear picture of what—I mean who—I'm looking at. Sorry, it must seem strange to you. This isn't the first time this habit has gotten me into trouble."

"Forget it," Karen replied, wondering just what he wanted to get a clear picture of. "I can't think of anything to tell about, why don't you go first?"

"OK, if you like, but you still have to take a turn." Stephen shifted his weight, trying to find a more comfortable position. Looking directly at Karen, but making sure he only looked at her face, he began. "It was a beautiful night as we sat around the campfire telling stories. The sun had set, and to the west the sky was a deep purple. It was a shade of purple that I've never seen anywhere else. The pines surrounding the clearing were like silhouettes, as if they had been cut from black paper." Stephen's voice trailed off as he became lost in his own thoughts. He remembered the cool dampness that settled around them making the fire seem all the warmer on their faces. He pictured the others telling stories, the stories brightening and dying like the flames in the fire. A new branch would catch and burn brightly for a moment, then flicker out, then another branch would catch from the embers of the old. The cadence of the flames was uneven, as the bright areas moved around the fire. So too, did the telling of the stories follow the cadence of the fire. A story would burn brightly for a moment, then flicker out, but the embers of that story would ignite another...

"Stephen!" Karen said, interrupting his thoughts. "You were telling about the stories around the campfire!"

"Yes, well—so we spent the night, stories moving around the

campfire like the flames in the fire."

Karen wondered if the stories were hot like the flames, but didn't feel like asking. Instead she remarked, "Were the stories interesting?"

"My cousin's wife was the only woman on a church baseball team, but she could hit and catch as well as the men. This was back when women weren't accepted in team sports, especially with men, but since this was a church team, anyone who wanted to play, could play. Of course, the men discouraged women from joining, so my cousin's wife sat on the bench for most of the games. She was stubborn enough to stick it out, but before the last game of the season she had it out with the captain. 'Look,' she said. 'If God made me as good as you men, He sure didn't intend for me to warm this bench every game. Who are you to deny the use of a God given talent? I think God would take that as an insult.' I guess that got his attention because he played her the whole last game. The men on the other team didn't expect a woman to hit so hard, so when they moved in, she belted it over their heads. When they moved out, she hit short. It turned out she caught the winning out, and their team won the championship. Even after all that the captain wouldn't acknowledge her. When the banquet was held to present the trophies to each team member, the figures on the trophies turned out to be women! Someone had made a mistake when they ordered them, but his wife told her captain it was the hand of God that directed the switch."

That was a harmless enough story, Karen thought, somewhat less apprehensive, but I'm sure he will eventually come around to off-color stories. He wasn't looking at her now, but staring at some far away point. "Would you like me to tell a story now?" she tendered.

Stephen, abruptly turning to face her, shook his head. "I'd like to tell one more story first, on a somewhat different subject, if that's OK with you. I sense the mood changing and I'd like to follow the change."

If the mood was changing, Karen didn't sense it. Here it comes, she thought with a sigh. She hurriedly tried to think of a plan of action if he started coming on to her. I'll move as far as possible from him, she thought. I'll say I have no interest in older men. I'll suggest that he might be more comfortable with a woman his own age. I'll scream if that doesn't work.

"Sure, I'd like to hear another story," Karen replied to Stephen's query, as she felt the hairs rise on the back of her neck.

"Why don't you sit down and relax," Stephen said, noticing her discomfort and thinking it was due to standing too long. "When you're settled, I'll begin."

Karen moved into the farthest corner from Stephen, drew her legs up close to herself, and motioned for him to start.

"That same night around the campfire I told this story about my grandmother. They all liked it, and I think you will too. When my grandmother was young, people believed all sorts of crazy stories. A dropped knife or an itchy palm meant company was coming. It seems that someone had told my grandmother that if the toe of a snoring man was pinched, he would answer any question he was asked. That seems pretty silly today, but remember my grandmother was only ten, and it wasn't much nuttier than the other stories she had heard. Grandma's older sister, Mandy, and her husband, Tom, were staying with the family and Tom was an awful snorer. My grandmother and her sister, Cora, slept in one bed across from the attic room that Mandy and Tom slept in. My grandmother was full of the Devil when she was young, and Cora was a close second. Grandma didn't have any trouble talking Cora into sneaking into the room across the hall and seeing if the story was true." Stephen stretched his legs out in front of himself, and settled back, obviously enjoying telling the story. "The next night, after her brother-in-law was snoring loudly, my grandmother and Cora crept silently into the next bedroom. Beds in those days were high off of the ground so both of them could easily fit underneath. My grandmother carefully reached under the covers at the bottom of the bed, waited for the next snore, and pinched the first big toe she found—hard. Well—all hell broke loose. Her older sister jumped out of bed, screaming that someone had grabbed her toe. The noise woke up my grandmother's mother, who ran up the stairs to find her daughter hollering and dancing around on the floor, and her son-in-law sitting bolt upright in bed staring with disbelief at his wife. I guess it took quite a while for her to calm down. Grandma and Cora laid low under the bed, and were pretty frightened at first as her mother was free with the switch. Then they started laughing, and held each other's mouth so they would-n't be discovered. Grandma laughed so hard she wet her pants. Later, when everyone had gone back to sleep, they snuck back into their bedroom. Cora pried up a loose board and Grandma stuck the wet pants under it. Her mother never did figure out where those pants went to, and Grandma and Cora never told. Years later, I asked my grandmother if that night had taught her and Cora a lesson, but I guess it didn't as they got into trouble on a regular basis until they grew up. Well, I've talked enough now, why don't you tell a story?"

Karen looked at Stephen without replying, but he didn't notice as he was looking out again at some distant point. She didn't know what to make of him. She had expected some type of come-on, not a cute story about his grandmother. She felt at a loss for words.

"Come on," Stephen added, "it will help to pass the time if we both take part. I'm hoping your stories will be more interesting than mine. You're awfully quiet. Were my stories so bad?"

Stephen was now looking at her with his questioning eyes, and Karen was beginning to feel uneasy once again. Just as she was starting to stammer out a reply, the elevator gave a shudder, then sprang to life. In a moment the doors were opened, and anxious voices were asking a jumble of questions. In the midst of the confusion Stephen turned to Karen. "Thanks for helping me pass the time in such an interesting way," he said in a louder than normal voice. "This Saturday, the department is having its annual hike. Janet tells me you like the outdoors, and it's a good way to meet people."

What a confusing man, Karen thought. I just don't know what to make of him.

As Stephen turned and left, several people faced toward Karen. "Oh, I'm used to entertaining in elevators," Karen said nonchalantly, stepping away from them. Feeling herself starting to blush Karen bowed to her audience, then walked quickly away.

CHAPTER FIVE

LUCID DREAMS

"YOU DREAM, DON'T YOU?" Karen, startled by Stephen's remark, didn't reply. "I can tell by the way you're looking out over the mountains and valleys," Stephen continued wistfully. "You have that look in your eye of someone who is planning where they will fly tonight—in your sleep."

"I hardly ever dream," Karen said, purposely avoiding his eyes.

Stephen shifted his position on the rock he was sitting on, looked back over the mountains and valleys, and continued. "Some people can dream in a very special way. It's a dream where the dreamer, that's you, realizes she is dreaming. That's the key, the realization that it is a dream, and not real, so the dream can become more than real."

"What?" Karen interjected.

"By realizing non-reality, super reality becomes possible," Stephen went on. "Now, the dreamer is able to control her dream. They're called lucid dreams. A common experience most lucid dreamers share is flying. Some lucid dreamers start by hopping off the ground in progressively longer jumps. Suddenly, instead of falling back to the ground, they start flying. Other people learn to fly at will, without having to work up to it by jumping. Some people may only have one lucid dream in their whole lifetime, while a few lucky people will lucid dream almost every night. How often do you lucid dream?"

"It's something that I've done my whole life," Karen admitted, idly moving little stones into patterns with her hands. "When I was small, I used to wake up in the mornings when my dad left for work. Not having to get up yet, I would drift back to sleep. I'd almost always dream, and they would be like you described, lucid dreams, but I never knew what to call them until now. I guess I thought it was something everyone did."

"No," Stephen said turning to look at Karen. "Lucid dreams are not that common. You're a lucky woman if you can lucid dream that easily."

"Later, as I grew older," Karen continued with her story, "I found I could dream even at night, but the best dreams came after I went back to sleep in the mornings. On Sunday morning I set the alarm to wake up early, then when I fall back asleep, I can have an hour or more to dream. You're right about what I was looking at. I like to climb to high places, look out over the view, fixing the valleys, the mountains, the rivers, and the whole sweep of the land in my mind so I can use those images for flying in my dreams."

Karen paused, thinking Stephen would want to reply. However, he was staring off into space, lost in thought. Karen wondered about Stephen. How could he have been perceptive enough to know that she lucid dreamed? She had never told anyone, except a close school friend. Thinking back on it, she wasn't even sure her friend fully understood what she was telling her. Could he have checked on my past somehow? Karen thought. Karen dismissed that thought as crazy, but it nevertheless disturbed her. Could it be a lucky guess? She didn't know.

Stephen returned from whatever thoughts of his own he was lost in. "Tell me about your lucid dreams," he said to Karen. "Are they vivid and real? Are they different from your regular dreams?"

"Oh—there's no comparison between my regular dreams and my lucid dreams!" Karen said excitedly. "Apart from being able to control the course of my lucid dreams, the clarity and colors are so vivid that everything seems more real—more real than real! It's not easy to describe, but it's true! Everything seems more real than real seems. I'll start out in a regular dream, then when the dream changes into a lucid dream, the colors just seem to explode. Even after all my years of dreaming, it still makes me catch my breath when it happens. I—I can't describe it any better than that, but that didn't describe it—not like it really is."

"Don't bother to try," Stephen broke in. "Someone who has never lucid dreamed will never understand, no matter how clearly you describe it. Someone who lucid dreams, well—they know. Another experience in lucid dreams, but less common than flying, is sexual. Did you know that climaxes that occur during lucid dreams are as real as regular ones that happen when people are awake; that the body has the same physical reactions? Lucid dream researchers are always looking for subjects who can dream on a regular basis. I know of several researchers who would like to study you. One works at the Sexual Response Clinic. Would you like to be a subject? Could I give him your name?"

Karen felt embarrassed and threatened, as if the most personal part of her life was being violated. Not wanting Stephen to know how this part of the conversation was affecting her, she turned her face into the shade, away from his gaze. "No," Karen replied, trying to sound detached and professional, like she thought a scientist should sound. "I don't think I would have the time, but I'll consider doing it in the future. Don't give my name out now, wait until I have the time, but—the study sounds interesting. Do you often fly in your lucid dreams?" Karen asked, hoping to change the subject back to flying.

"Oh, let's not talk about my dreams, I already know about them. Let's talk about yours. Do you ever have sexual experiences?" Stephen persisted.

"I fly, that's all," Karen replied, still trying to sound professional.

In spite of the shadows on her face, Stephen noticed the color rising in her cheeks. He was sure the real answer wasn't the one she wanted him to believe, but not wanting to press the question, he continued. "Tell me about the strangest lucid dream that you ever had," he said.

"My strangest lucid dream?" Karen thought, relieved she could change the subject away from sexual experiences. "Let me think. There have been so many, but one particular dream was the most fascinating of all. I was flying, as I always do, with my hands outstretched, soaring over a beautiful valley at dusk. I glided over several houses, but one house in particular caught my eye. It was the single lighted window that I first noticed. I can still remember the wind and how it blew my hair back from my face as I turned and flew down for a closer look. I landed silently on the ground outside of the window. I moved forward and looked in, and I could see the outline of a man's head and shoulders inside. The man was sitting on a bed, bending down to take off his socks. It was strange. The minute I saw him bending over, I knew everything about him. All his past experiences, his thoughts, everything. The funny thing was that all this didn't seem strange in my dream. It seemed as natural as knowing how to walk. Then I turned and flew off. I've hoped to have the experience again, but I've never been able to."

"I'm not surprised," Stephen returned. "Most of us can't explain how we do the amazing things we do. A great artist can't explain his talent, anymore than a musician can. Some people can tell the day of the week any date will fall on. Ask them how and they'll tell you they don't know. We are the most amazing when we don't have to think about what we do. That is when our talent flows. Don't try so hard to have the same experience. For you, such a talent may be as natural as seeing. Talking to you like this has given me an idea."

"An idea?" asked Karen.

"Yes! An idea that I have been wanting to try for a long, long time. Now I believe that you can help me with it. Would you like to help me?"

Even though Stephen was trying to be casual, Karen sensed a tension in his voice he couldn't hide. Karen cautiously replied, "I suppose—what did you have in mind?"

"You said that you always lucid dream on Sundays, in the morning?"

"Oh no, not every Sunday," Karen quickly replied. "I'm not as good a lucid dreamer as you think," she added.

"Tomorrow," Stephen went on, ignoring her reluctance. "Tomorrow, fly over that town in the valley to the right. A clothing store is a few doors down on the main street. Fly in the door and stand in front of the clothing racks. Move down the racks until one article of clothing begins to shimmer. Stop there and stare at it as it shimmers. That's all. It's simple. Yes, I think that should do it. Set your alarm for 3 a.m., that will give us plenty of time."

Us? Karen thought. "No—I don't think so," Karen slowly answered. "I don't think I want to go fly over that town. I want to fly somewhere else. Actually I've been thinking of flying over another landscape that I saw in a travel show. I'll fly there on Sunday. That is, if I even lucid dream."

"Sure," Stephen replied, disappointment in his voice. "It wouldn't have worked anyway. Let's forget I even asked and enjoy the rest of the hike."

The rest of the hike was pleasant enough for Karen. She loved being outdoors, and the mountains were one of her favorite places. She and Stephen talked off and on as they walked, but stayed away from lucid dreams. On the trail back, Karen was able to separate from the others and find some time to talk with Gary. "What have you been able to find out about Jim Fulton's hidden files?" she asked, when they were out of hearing from most of the group.

"Maybe something, maybe nothing," Gary shrugged. "But, I just can't get the fact out of my head that every scrambled station report started with the same false station identifier. Why was that? Was someone trying to mark those lines on purpose? I'll admit that this is a far out crazy idea, but could someone be sending messages in some sort of code? The same station identifier would mark the lines for decoding. The next letter or number might tell what program to run to decode the message. That is, if they are really sophisticated about it.

"Interesting," Karen thoughtfully replied. "Then someone would just have to scan the station reports and pull out the key ones."

"Sure, but it could all be done by computer. The computer could be programmed to copy all the false station reports from the main list into another file. A continuation of the program could decode them. Everything could be done in one program so that only the decoded message was printed out. It could be that simple."

"Is there a way to decode the messages if we don't know the programs?" Karen asked in a low voice.

"There are programs floating around on the network, if a person knows where to look, that can break codes. But, it's almost impossible if the code is changed often. Sometimes, some words remain coded the same even if the coding scheme is changed. If that is true, than we can at least recover some of the message. These code breaking programs can take days to run. The more samples of the code we have, the better chance we have to break it. I guess we can always hope that whoever did the coding was lazy, and didn't change it too often."

"Can you do it?" Karen asked in the same low voice.

"I'm way ahead of you there. I've had a program running for days, with no luck as of the time I left for this hike. If this idea is all off the wall, then lots of computer time will be burned up for nothing. I've written a program to check all the current station reports for the same odd station name. If the program finds any, they will be added to the list that Fulton made which will add to the chances of breaking the code."

"Don't tell Stephen about what you are doing," Karen whispered. "He thinks all my suspicions about Jim Fulton's disappearance are nonsense."

"Anything I do on my own time is my own business," Gary replied rather loudly. "No one controls my time, but myself!"

"I'm sure of that," soothed Karen, surprised at how agitated he had become. "By the way, how do you know so much about computers?"

"I pick things up here and there," Gary said, sounding less agitated.

Karen started to ask another question just as Stephen walked up beside them. "I hope that you two are not talking about business on such a beautiful day," Stephen remarked, in a half serious and half joking manner.

"Not at all," Karen said, not looking into his eyes. "Gary wanted to know the name of the purple flowers on the edge of the trail.

Do you know their name?"

"No, I don't think I do. I'm surprised Gary is interested in anything but his computers," Stephen casually remarked.

That night, when Karen returned home, she thought about the conversation she'd had with Stephen. "No way am I going to help him with his study, whatever it is!" Karen said out loud. "I'll fly where I want to tonight. Gary's right. My own time is my own! Stephen has no business asking me to help him on my own time!"

Karen thought about the hike, Stephen, Gary, and Fulton while she was getting ready for bed. Karen almost didn't set her alarm, but at the last moment decided to lucid dream in spite of Stephen. Karen set the alarm for 3 a.m.. He doesn't own the day or night, Karen thought. I can lucid dream that time if I want to—he can have his own dreams!

When the alarm woke her at 3 a.m., Karen felt as if she had hardly slept. Her sleep was filled with disjointed dreams of codes she had to break, sinister people, murdered students. As soon as she turned the alarm off, she fell back into a fitful sleep. Soon she was flying over the valley she had committed to memory on the hike. Flying in her lucid dreams gave her a feeling of peace she rarely found in her waking life. As she flew lower over the valley, Karen noticed a building with lighted windows. Thinking she might be able to repeat her past lucid dream, she moved closer to the door. It was a clothing store. Dreams have a way of lessening caution, and so it was for Karen. She stepped inside. Racks of clothing covered the walls. Karen moved slowly down the racks, fascinated by the bright colors and patterns. I'm doing what Stephen wanted, and I shouldn't, she realized, as shivers started moving up her neck. She stopped and started to turn back, but a piece of clothing caught her eye as she hurried out of the door. It was shimmering. Karen tried to turn away, but its strange beauty held her transfixed.

As she moved closer to the dress and reached out to touch it her hand disappeared into the shimmering colors. Reaching out to find her hand she stepped into the colors and suddenly was propelled forward into darkness. She was traveling with tremendous speed. When it seemed she could accelerate no faster, Karen abruptly stopped. She found herself sitting on a bench at the edge of a beautiful verdant field. The color of the grass was so vivid, Karen could see each individual blade. She sat spellbound.

"Welcome, Karen, to my lucid dream," a voice from behind her said.

CHAPTER SIX

PEARLS

KAREN TURNED TO SEE Stephen standing behind her. "I wanted you to come," Stephen said, as he moved to sit beside her. Stephen slowly turned towards her and he reached out and took her hands in his. He drew her hands to his chest, gently placing them over his heart.

"Feel my heart, Karen. Feel it beat. I'm real and alive! You're real and alive, and we're here—together! Don't give up this moment— this unbelievable moment and wake. Come with me. Let me show you my special dream world. You're the only one I've ever invited to share it. Would you—would you let me share it with you?"

Karen couldn't understand whose hands were pressed against Stephen's chest. She could feel his heart beating, but her hands— they were under her bed covers. She wondered how she could feel his heart if her hands were safe at home. She felt her head on her pillow and the sheets around her neck. Who is replying to Stephen? she thought. Is it another Karen, another Karen not safe in bed?

"Yes," the other Karen slowly said. "Yes, I would very much like to see your dream world." Karen heard the words come from her lips, but her voice was different, so she thought it wasn't her. She was in

43

bed, not here. She felt detached, as if she was only an observer, here to only take notes, to watch them and record. If I only watch them, she thought, it will be all right.

Stephen seemed not to have noticed anything strange about her answer. Stephen looked directly into Karen's eyes. "I'm glad you're here," he said in a voice edged with anticipation. "I've felt that my dream world was too beautiful to keep to myself, but I've never found anyone who was capable of coming with me until I saw you gazing over the valley. I knew you didn't want to come when I asked you on the hike, but I hoped when you were dreaming, the beauty and wonder of it all would draw you to me. In the morning we can tell ourselves that this was only a dream. But now you're here! With me! Come, explore this dream, for the morning will soon overtake us!"

Stephen gently placed Karen's hands into her lap, turned and walked into the field. As Karen stood up to follow him, the two Karens—the observer, and the one sleeping safely in her bed— became one. She looked down at her hands. They were her hands. When she called out to Stephen, it was her voice! She was Karen! She was here! It was breathtaking.

Tall stalks of grass reached up to Karen's shoulders. Patches of shorter grasses were mixed with areas of soft, green moss. The colors of green were dazzling in their depth of shade. The soft moss was cool and pleasant on her bare feet. The grasses brushed against her legs and arms. Their touch felt like the softest caresses as they slipped by. The tallest bent to touch her breasts and lips and lingered there for a moment before passing. "Don't be frightened by the grass, Karen," Stephen called back. "You're a child of nature, and she likes to admire her creations—be glad she approves of you."

Karen, too lost in her sensations to reply, walked after Stephen.

Ahead the grasses opened onto a bed of wild flowers. Their scent blew towards Karen, carried by a warm breeze. Reaching the flowers first, Stephen bent down, and, picking up a handful, turned back towards Karen. "She loves these flowers," he said, holding them up in the breeze. "She loves them wild as they grow, with no plan save beauty, just as she loves you, who also grows with no plan save beauty." He reached towards her, placing the flowers carefully, to make neat rows in the garden of her hair. He placed a row of flowers along her breasts, their heads peeking out of the bodice of her nightgown and nodding with the rhythm of her breathing. Stray petals fell at her feet and covered them with fragrance. "Come!" he urged as he reached out his hand. "We need to reach those hills in the distance, and we have other things to see on the way."

Karen took his hand. His grip was firm as they walked together. She was aware of so many sensations at once—the flowers, the field, Stephen walking beside her. The soft touch of the grasses had made her aware of her body in a way she had never before experienced. She felt alive, free, and happy—very happy. She felt attractive for the first time in her life. Karen walked along, transfixed by the vista before her. Rolling green hills rose behind the field, backed by snow-covered mountains. White, lazy, cumulus clouds floated along the peaks. Everything was bathed in the fresh morning sun. Almost to herself, Karen wondered out loud, "The grass and moss are so soft on my feet—are there no rough patches or thorns in your dream?"

"I've thought about that," Stephen replied as he broke into her thoughts. "Have you ever read the Devil and Daniel Webster?"

"I think so. Was that the story where Daniel Webster captures the Devil, or something like that?"

"Yes, he tricks the Devil into turning himself into a moth, then he captures the Devil in a box, or something like a box. I can't exactly remember myself. Now, this is what I never could understand. Why does Daniel let the Devil go at the end of the story? Imagine! Daniel Webster had all the evil in the world trapped, and he freed it. I couldn't understand it, I just couldn't!"

"I never thought of the story in that way," Karen remarked, "but I can understand why you were upset."

"Later," Stephen continued, "only when I was older did I realize why he had done it. We couldn't enjoy a world with no evil in it. Doesn't the sun seem brighter after the storm, joy more precious after sorrow? Only when we have suffered a great loss, can we experience great love. Our joy can only rise as high as the depth of our sorrow."

"Why then," Karen asked, "are there no thorns in your grass? Won't it seem softer after the thorns?"

Stephen drew a breath. He continued to gaze out towards the mountains. He went several steps further, then he stopped. Stephen slowly moved his hands along the tops of the grasses, lost in his thoughts. He finally answered Karen, but he was speaking away from her, as if to the distant hills. "In the world—not here, but the one we live in—there is enough sorrow and unhappiness to make up for all the thorns that are missing from my dream world. Oh, Karen," Stephen sighed, turning back towards her. "We'll find more than enough thorns in the morning!"

Gradually the grasses became shorter. The last of the tall stocks bent to touch her breasts, then waved as if to nod good-bye as they drew away. The short grasses gave way to moss. The moss deepened in color. Just as the color became so deep that Karen was afraid to step forward for fear she would plunge into the color and disappear, the moss stopped at the edge of a still pond. Stephen let go of her hand, slipped his nightshirt off, and glided beneath the waters.

When his head broke the surface he turned to face her. He didn't say a word, but only looked into her eyes, then turned and slipped under the water again. Karen slipped her nightgown over her head and set it down on the moss by the edge of the pond. Moving quickly she slid into the water before Stephen resurfaced. The cool water brought her senses to a peak as it reached for her body and embraced it. "This is how we were meant to be," she thought, "free from the world, naked before nature." She rolled on her back and let the water flow over her breasts. Little whirls spread away from her nipples and rippled toward the edges, gently lapping at the moss bordering the pond. Stephen broke the surface beside her. "Have you seen the bottom? I think you will like it," he said, shaking the water from his hair.

Karen dove toward the bottom. The flowers in her hair floated away on the surface in tiny whirlpools. A miniature forest spread out before her. The forest swayed to the currents in a gentle rhythm. Hiding between the plants were colorful fish, streaked by the sunlight filtering down in beams from the surface. Karen was so fascinated by the scene that Stephen had to remind her to surface. As their heads reached the air, Karen was filled with the earthy smell of the moss-ringed pond. "Could heaven be any nicer!" Karen exclaimed.

Stephen swam to the edge and climbed out. Karen, unashamed, looked at his naked body, wet and shiny from the swim. Her eyes followed the course of the water as it formed droplets that ran off his face and neck, over his chest, and down across his thighs.

Stephen motioned for her to come beside him. She purposely stepped onto the shore in full view. She wanted him to see her. She stood facing him, her legs resting easily apart. Stephen, in turn, looked fully at her, his eyes lazily drifting over her. Karen noticed that some drops had fallen onto the delicate curls of hair below

Stephen's waist. Karen reached out and took one of the drops on her finger.

"Little pearls," said Karen, "to adorn your manliness. Each pearl for a child to be born. Each pearl for a lover to come."

"Are there pearl drops on me, Stephen?" Karen asked, keeping her lips slightly apart as she spoke. "Is there one for each of my children to be, for each of my lovers?"

Not answering her question, Stephen looked directly at her, but his voice had a distant sound. "I've seen much of the beauty of the world. I've gazed at the Taj Mahal at sunrise, from the very window its creator was imprisoned behind. I've sat on the beaches of the Pacific Coast at the very moment the sun dips below the horizon, and caught the fleeting flash of green rays. I've seen the mark of a bird's wing in the fresh snow, the tracks of seabirds in the sand. But in all my travels I have never seen anything as beautiful as a woman. Never! The way each line flows together is beyond description. Such form is found nowhere else in creation and it's a beauty meant to be touched! Have you ever seen the life of a rose? As it grows older and its petals fade and wither, its beauty moves into the rose hip at the base of the flower. All the beauty of the rose is now within the hip, but it is there if you look for it. As a woman ages, her beauty also moves inside. Like the rose, her beauty is still there if you look past the faded petals. Oh, Karen! Don't ever quit looking for the beauty that will still be inside you as you age!" Stephen was still looking directly into her eyes, but now he spoke in a softer voice, and his words swept around her. "Karen, when the first man drew the first woman on cave walls—that woman was you. When the first great master set a woman down in oils—that woman was you. All through the centuries, the woman that men desire—was you. Strong legs and thighs, full hips, smooth round curves—that woman was you. That combination of softness and strength, like the feel of velvet-covered chains, has inspired men forever. Now you are before me in all your beauty. Thank you— thank you for being that woman!"

Karen had been weaving a chain of flowers and wild grasses while Stephen was speaking. She slowly moved closer to him. She leaned forward, letting her breasts brush against him. Without speaking, Karen tied the chain around his waist. She moved her hands slowly down over the chain and onto the pearl drops of water. "Don't I excite you, Stephen?" Karen asked in a small, questioning voice. "Is something the matter?"

"Oh Karen. Tonight I will not be your lover. She understands you better than I, and she demands to be the first. There, on that higher hill she waits for you. There she waits for me to bring you to her."

They walked side by side, her hand in his, each silent in thought. Occasionally, Stephen brushed against her, which made Karen's desire for him more intense. "This lover, how does she know so much about me?" Karen asked, breaking the silence.

"You're a woman of the rich smell of the forest. A woman whom the sun loves to warm, whose hair the wind likes to gently play with. The sun and the wind know their own."

Still holding hands, they moved up the hill with easy strides. The hillside was covered with tiny purple flowers. They had grown so tightly together that they felt like a carpet to Karen. "These flowers made this bed only for you, Karen," Stephen said as he motioned for her to lie down. He held her hands as she lay back. The carpet of flowers was cool, like the moss had been under her feet. She rested her head on her hands, her legs were slightly bent, and her back fit the curve of the hill. "Your lover-to-be knew you would come, but now she wants me to leave. Good-bye, Karen."

LUCID DREAMS

It seemed to Karen that she lay forever looking up at the deep blue of the sky. Her body felt alive in a way she had never experienced before. She could feel every flower petal beneath her, each cool petal was like a soft kiss. As she became lost in the sensation of each petal's touch, a warm breeze began to stir around her legs. The breeze swirled around her ankles before slowly and ever so gently touching her calves. The breeze moved over the curves of her legs, taking the tension away as it slowly whirled. The breeze repeatedly subsided, only to begin again stronger. Each time it began, the wind moved further up Karen's legs. Soon the wind was stroking her thighs, finding each tiny, golden hair and caressing it in turn. Then it stopped. Minutes went by. Karen was faint with anticipation. When the wind started, it now moved, ebbing and flowing along the insides of her legs. As it reached higher, the wind moved away and outward over her hips. When the wind again died, Karen slid forward, inviting the wind to return. This time, the wind returned with a stronger hand. The touches were more than Karen could bear, and she heard herself crying out to the wind. "Take me! Finish me now! No more! I can't bear it!"

But the wind carried away her words.

She felt the sun's rays concentrate on her breasts, then close upon her nipples. Warmer and warmer until her nipples burned. The wind continued its motion, as more rays moved along her legs. Now the sun's rays were different as they felt hard against her. Upward and upward they came, as Karen pressed down towards them. The wind lifted her away from the ground with a strong gust. She felt her hair fall behind her as the wind caught her under the curve of her back. Suddenly, the warmth of the sun thrust hard inside her. She pushed against the warmth with all her strength. The warmth moved upward, deeper and deeper inside, penetrating her very being. The warmth became very intense, flowing outward from her pelvis in waves of pleasure that washed over her. She tried to call out, but her voice was gone.

Karen sat upright in her bed. Her covers had been thrown off and were tangled around her legs. She was soaked with sweat. Her hands trembled as she tried to stand. Shaking all over, Karen collapsed, falling back onto the sheets. When she awoke again, the sun was shining through the window, shafts of light falling over her. Karen carefully eased herself out of bed, away from the shafts. She half expected them to follow, but the light was still. As she dressed, she ran her hands over her body, looking for some trace of the night before. But Karen found none. "A dream!" Karen said to herself, "It was only a dream! But, what a wonderful, wonderful dream—only I wish it hadn't been with Stephen!"

Karen passed Stephen in the hall Monday morning. He acted as if nothing had happened. He said "Good morning" in his usual way. Karen replied, "Good morning" as she always did. When she reached her desk, she stared in disbelief. On top of it, in plain view, was a brand new copy of The Devil and Daniel Webster!

CHAPTER SEVEN

TIDAL CURRENTS

"SO DAD, where are we going today?" asked Andy as he came down the hall stairs, jumping over the last three, and landing with a thump in the entry. "It's Sunday—family day! The day we do fun stuff together!"

"Dad!" Jill called out from the kitchen. "Can't he be a little quieter first thing in the morning?"

"So it is family day," replied Stephen, reaching out and messing up Andy's hair with his hand. "What kind of fun stuff shall we do today?"

"Well—I like parks, the zoo, the locks, walking on the waterfront is fun—a ferry ride is nice—but I want to go to the tidal basin," Andy answered. "Old Professor Greenly told me that he sometimes finds Indian arrowheads at low tide. He thinks the river washes them into the tidal basin. Guess what? The tide is lowest about two hours from now. Could we go?"

"I don't see why not," Stephen barely said before Jill burst into the room.

"Dad!" she exclaimed. "We aren't going to do what Andy wants again, are we? I always thought he was your favorite, but can't you think of me first, for once! Why do we always have to do what 'King Boy' wants? Old Town is having the monthly Gallery Walk, and I'd love to go!"

"Dad! You said we could go to the tidal basin!" Andy whined.

"Dad! You always put Andy first!"

"OK, OK," interrupted Stephen. "What time does the Gallery Walk close?"

"Six p.m." Jill answered.

"Good! We can do both!" Stephen replied, relieved that he could avoid another conflict. "We'll leave now and have about three hours at the tidal basin, then we'll still have plenty of time to go on the Gallery Walk. Take your boots, and good shoes for later. We'll eat dinner out. Let's go do some fun stuff!"

The tidal basin was between his home and the University where Stephen worked. The Rushing River plunged out of the mountains east of the University, then widened and slowed as it meandered through lush wetlands. The wetlands gave way to a tidal basin as the river narrowed and swept through a deep channel into a saltwater sound. Fresh water flowed into the sound unimpeded at low tide, but on an incoming tide saltwater flowed against the current of the river creating deadly currents. Farms once stood along the shores of the tidal basin, flourishing on the rich top soil deposited by past floods. All that was left now were a few crumbling buildings and toppled fences. Ten years earlier the tidal basin and adjacent wetlands were declared a protected area. The only structures allowed to remain were the Tidal Basin Road Draw Bridge which spanned the channel, and several maintenance buildings.

Looking out of the car window as they drove along, Andy's thoughts turned to old Professor Greenly. "Hey Dad! Do you think Professor Greenly will be there today? It seems like he's always there. Doesn't he have a home?"

"He does," Stephen replied, maneuvering around a rut in the road. "But, I don't think he spends much time there. His whole life has been devoted to studying the tidal basin, its currents, and the creatures that live there. He is very interested in the adaptation of tidal life to the surges of saltwater and how the currents affect this adaptation. You see the surges of saltwater, they—"

"Dad," broke in Jill, not interested in hearing a lecture about the tidal basin. "Would you like to hear what galleries are having special shows?" Not waiting for a reply, Jill quickly started reading from the Gallery Guide. "The Hansen Gallery is having a special showing of glass paintings. The Corner Gallery is featuring a revival of landscape and period romantic paintings. Here's something different. The Back Alley Gallery is hosting a show called 'Beauty in Death.' Let's see—'Photographs and drawings of people at the moment of death. Several famous paintings of dead game, and some war drawings and pictures.' Now that's different."

"It sounds gruesome to me," Stephen remarked. "I think I'll pass on that one."

"Sounds like neat stuff to me," Andy chimed in. "I'll go with Jill, and you can wait outside. Will you take me, Jill?"

"Sure," Jill replied, "I guess an artist should be interested in all art. This will expand my artistic viewpoint."

"You can expand your viewpoint all you want," Stephen cut in, "It still sounds gruesome to me."

As the road drew nearer to the tidal basin, houses gradually became few and far between. By the time they could see the Tidal Basin Road Draw Bridge, no houses were left. A few pleasure boats were passing under the bridge as they moved along the river. A lone figure in a small boat was bending over something in the water.

"Hey, that might be old Professor Greenly!" Andy exclaimed as he pointed downstream of the bridge. "Let's get closer and see! Look! I'm sure that's him. It's the University skiff. I can tell by the markings on the side. Can we get closer Dad?"

Stephen pulled the car onto the side of the road into a parking area used by the bridge tender. A set of old stairs led downward under the bridge onto a dirt path which trailed the edge of the channel. Before the tidal basin had been declared a nature area, the path had been well kept. Now blackberries, vine maple, and nettles had overgrown it in places. "Watch your step," Stephen cautioned, as they carefully made their way downstream toward the old professor. "We'll try to reach the point to the left, then, if we're lucky, we can get his attention from there."

Several minutes later, Stephen, Andy, and Jill stood on the small point jutting out towards the river. Loose dirt and cave-ins along the path made travel further out on the point impossible.

"That's him, all right," Andy said. "See! He's wearing his old hat. But why is he slumped over the side?"

Stephen leaned forward, cupped his hands around his mouth and yelled, "Professor Greenly, Professor Greenly, hello!" He received no reply.

"Do you think something could be the matter with him—he's not moving?" Jill asked in a worried voice.

All three started yelling towards the skiff in unison, but the figure still didn't move. "I'm sure he's OK," Stephen broke in. "I'd feel better, though, if we could get his attention! I think we should alert the bridge tender." Just as they started to climb back toward the bridge, the bridge whistle blew in response to a sailboat approaching the channel. At the sound of the whistle, the old professor straightened up and turned toward the bridge. When he saw Stephen and the children looking at him, he waved.

"Boy!" exclaimed Stephen, "I've forgotten how hard of hearing these old professors can be!"

Professor Greenly motioned for them to meet him upstream of the bridge where the outgoing tide had uncovered strips of muddy beach. It was three quarters of an hour before they had made their way carefully along the channel, climbed the stairs, changed into their boots, and made their way to the beach where Professor Greenly patiently waited. Stepping slowly out of the skiff, the professor greeted them warmly. "Well—have you come to see an old man at work, or does the chance of finding Indian arrowheads bring you here?" With a deft movement he reached behind Andy's ear. "You haven't been doing a very good job of washing behind those ears, young man! Look! What's this?" he said as he pulled an arrowhead from behind Andy's ear. "And—what's this?" he laughed as he pulled another one from the other ear.

"Check my ears again!" cried Andy, looking down at the perfect shapes in his hand.

"If you want more, try digging along that beach where I dug this morning," the old professor said, pointing towards a narrow strip of mud dug up in several places. "Put your sister and dad to work too. Is it fun that brings you here today?"

"For us it's fun, but what brings you here on Sunday?" Stephen asked.

"A puzzle," Professor Greenly answered, "a darn confusing puzzle. I've been studying this channel and tidelands for years. I've got 15 current meters that I've run for more years than I can remember, but now they show that the tidal currents are changing. Maybe the channel has changed naturally from erosion at the bottom, but I don't think so. The bottom and sides of the channel are mostly rock, so that doesn't seem possible. I guess I don't know, I really don't know."

"Could erosion up or downstream of the channel cause the changes in the current?" Stephen wondered.

Professor Greenly scratched his chin thoughtfully and stared at the river upstream of the bridge. "No—I really don't think so, but my puzzle is your gain. That narrow strip of mud that I was digging on has only been uncovered a few weeks."

"Why couldn't the changing beach, in some way influence the currents?" Stephen asked, still trying to think of reasons for the changes.

"It might be possible," the professor remarked, "but my model indicates that the beaches can't influence the currents. Only the currents can change the beaches. Have you seen my model? A bright young student adapted it for me from an existing model used for another channel."

"Is it a scale model with moving water and little jets of dye to trace the currents?" Andy broke in. "I saw one once in an old science book."

"Old is right!" the professor exclaimed. "This is the computer age. The only things that flow in this model are electrons. What an improvement over the old scale models built out of plaster and paint. It took days of careful work to change the shape of a channel. Now the same change can be done with a few hours of programming. However, the model is only as good as what I input, so I need to check the shape very carefully. I'm not going to be working too late tonight, however. I always like to quit before dark so I can see to load the skiff on the trailer. Would you like to stop by the University and see my model results?"

"Maybe we can," Stephen replied. "I promised Jill we'd go on the Gallery Walk after we dig for arrowheads. If we're not done too late, we'll stop by on the way home. I'll look for a light on in your office."

One hour of digging brought the treasure seekers two complete arrowheads and several broken pieces. On the way back to the car Stephen remarked to his children, "It's a shame that Professor Greenly is so old. I think he's going to retire as soon as his current grant runs out, sometime in the next few months. After he leaves, there won't be anyone to continue his work."

"How come, Dad?" asked Andy, clutching his treasures.

"Well, Andy," Stephen replied, "I just don't think there are any students interested in that kind of field work to follow him. The student helping him with the model is only part-time, and is interested in another project for his thesis, or so the professor tells me."

"At least he got to do what he enjoyed most of his life," Jill remarked as she watched the buildings of the city come closer in the distance.

"Tell us about Old Town, Dad," Jill inquired. "Is there any interesting history that you know about? It will make the time go faster."

"Old Town was once the main business district of Northport," Stephen began, "back when the town was rapidly growing from an explosion of fishing and logging companies around the turn of the century. With all that money flowing into town, storekeepers could afford to build buildings to last. Their dreams are still captured in the building names carved into solid granite over entrances, and on cornerstones. Slater Building, Gateway to Alaska; Thompson Building, Keyholder to the Northwest Passage. You know the Thompson Building? It is the one with the stone heads of walrus and polar bears on the facade—" Stephen paused in his story, and became silent for several minutes.

"What are you thinking about, Dad?" asked Andy. "Has something made you sad?"

"Oh, I was just thinking about the people who built those

buildings," Stephen said, pausing before he continued. "I picture them young and full of life, standing before the names, proud of what they created, full of hope for the future. Some had children —families—like us. I suppose they thought their children, and their children's children would reap the harvest of what they started. You know, some of the businesses only lasted one generation. The boom in lumber was over that fast."

"What happened?" interjected Andy, starting to pay more attention to what Stephen was relating.

"When the loggers first started cutting trees, giant Douglas fir grew everywhere. The loggers could fall them, and easily move them to nearby mills. Of course, they cut the closest ones first, and at a hectic pace. As the trees were cut further from town and the port, costs increased and profits declined."

"But Old Town is the nicest part of Northport. What happened?" Jill asked.

"Things we build, things that last, things that have a universal appeal which cuts across the generations have to survive middle age. It's their most dangerous time in life," Stephen mused.

"How so?" remarked Jill.

"When they are infants, they are new, and the newness protects them. As they reach adulthood, the newness has worn off, but they are still useful and survive. But by middle age, they are considered old-fashioned, and most people want modern things. You see, they have to be built to last, so they can survive a period of neglect, when the only people who want them are those who have no other choice. If they survive into old age, suddenly they become classics. What would the builders of Old Town think, if they could stand there today? The joke's on us, they'd think. They built to be modern, and—," Stephen trailed off. "Looks like we're here. I guess this lets you kids off the hook—for now."

Stephen turned onto a side street that abutted the street the Gallery Walk was held on. "Let's park here. We can walk to the start and not be caught in too much traffic when we leave."

The first gallery they went into was showing works of new artists. "Look at this painting, Dad," Jill said. "It's really interesting. Look how the colors blend together. What do you think?"

"I think Andy could do as well. What do you think Andy?"

"I've seen artwork in my class that would fit right in," Andy said. "Do you think anyone from my class has a painting here?"

"Hardly," Jill interrupted indignantly. "These are important artists, each selected for their contribution to new thinking in art. Some of these artists might well be famous someday! Keep that in mind!"

"Well Jill, I have a test that never fails to separate good art from bad," Stephen joined in. "It never fails. I call it the 'Garage Sale Test.' Take a painting, put it into a garage sale anywhere in America, along with all the other items for sale. Don't put any special marking on it. That's important in order for the test to be fair. If it sells before the end of the day, it's art. If not, toss it out with the rest of the leftover junk! It's that simple."

"Dad!" Jill sighed. "Thank heavens you don't control the art market! Let's try the next gallery. It's the Corner Gallery. In the guide, the show is listed as landscapes and period romantic paintings. We'll all like those."

Stephen, Jill, and Andy made their way down the street, through the different galleries. Jill was right. They all enjoyed the paintings at the Corner Gallery. Each of them found works in other galleries they also liked. The last gallery on the street was the Back Alley, named for its location on one of Old Town's more scenic alleys. The Back Alley was noted for its innovative showings. The reviews weren't always favorable, but the shows always drew a large and noisy crowd.

"Will you change your mind and come with Andy and me to the Back Alley?" Jill asked Stephen. "I don't think the show will be all that bad. I'd like you to come."

"No thank you, I don't think so," Stephen answered. "I don't care for shows about death—it gives me the creeps. You and Andy can tell me about the show on the way to the University. Don't take too long, OK? I told Professor Greenly we'd try to stop on the way home.

Both Jill and Andy were very quiet as Stephen drove away from Old Town. "How was the show?" he asked.

Jill looked over at Andy. He returned the look, but didn't speak. Jill shrunk further into the car seat, and looked out of the window.

"Was it that bad?" Stephen tried again.

"It wasn't the show—at least not all of it ," Andy finally spoke out.

"The show was OK," added Jill. "Some of the pictures were classics—pictures of game animals and birds hanging from cords. Those were fine. Harder to look at were the pictures of people that died peacefully in their sleep. I suppose they weren't so bad, as most of them looked so peaceful, almost serene. I guess there was beauty in their faces."

Tell Dad about the other ones," Andy broke in.

"Several photos showed people at the moment of violent deaths. They were pretty bad, but—," Jill trailed off, giving a small shudder.

"Are you cold, honey?" Stephen asked. "Do you want the heat turned on?"

"Tell dad about the man!" Andy said turning towards Jill.

Jill shuddered again. "There was this man. We saw him as we came in. He caught our eye right off. He was dressed all in black."

"Like an undertaker," Andy added.

Jill continued. "Like an undertaker. Only he wasn't tall, like movie undertakers. The next thing I noticed about him was his fingers. They were long—compared to his height, and very slender. They seemed too sensitive, too sensitive for the rest of his looks. We forgot about him while we looked at the older paintings. When we got to the last pictures, the violent ones, he was still standing there. He hadn't moved from the place he was in when we came in the door. He turned to face us as we approached. His eyes were cold and gray, but his voice was soft and low. 'Can you see the beauty?' he asked us. 'It's in the arch of the back, the perfect arc. Could any artist have drawn a better one?' I wasn't sure what he meant. He reached out his slender fingers and touched the photo, and traced the arc with his finger."

"He said something about the moment of the soul, or something like that," Andy took over. "It wasn't what he said, but how he said it. We nicknamed him Mr. Death after we left."

"Could you turn up the heat, Dad?" Jill asked. "I can't seem to warm up."

"Sure honey," Stephen replied. "Let's not let some creep spoil the rest of our day. Look! The light is on in Professor Greenly's office."

On Sunday the parking guards were gone, so they drove straight to the professor's building. They climbed the stairs, and finding the door ajar, called in. "Professor Greenly! May we come in? Receiving no answer, Stephen opened the door and looked in. The professor was sitting with his back to the door, his left arm lying on the arm of the chair. He was staring at a letter held in his left hand, his head resting in his right hand. His breathing seemed shallow and quick. Alarmed, Stephen hurried in. As they circled his chair, the professor looked up. "Forgive me for not answering the door, but I'm too surprised by this letter to act normally. It was in a pile of mail on my desk that I hadn't bothered to open yet. I just don't believe it. I thought I was too old, and my studies were over." He handed the letter to Stephen.

"It's from the Institute for the Environment, some foundation I guess." Stephen skimmed the letter. "They want you to come to New York as a consultant. They're impressed by your publication record and recent work. What does this mean, professor?"

"It means another year of work. They want me to bring my current meters. They want me to come as soon as possible, so I'll have to end my current research immediately. Their study is based in New York Harbor. They already have a computer model of the harbor so I won't be needing my own model. It seems a shame to let my computer sit here for the year I'm gone. Would you kids like to take care of it for me?"

"That'd be great professor," Andy replied. "Could you leave the model of the tidal basin on the computer. I might like to try it, for fun."

"I can," Professor Greenly returned. "However, I don't think you will be able to run it. Maybe I should take it off the hard drive and put it on a tape. That way, you would have more room for your own software. I'll do that if I have time."

On the way home after dinner, Andy and Jill were unusually quiet. Both of them were thinking about the odd and scary man they met at the Back Alley Gallery. "Do you want to keep this brochure from the show where we saw Mr. Death?" Andy asked Jill. When Jill shook her head, Andy tossed it into the litter bag.

Stephen was lost in his own thoughts. Quite the man, Professor Greenly, his career is not over, not yet. Karen?—will she come next week on Sunday morning? I hope so!

CHAPTER EIGHT

EXERCISES

THE DYING FLY made little swirls of dust which floated down from the light fixture onto the slender fingers. "Exercises, exercises, we must do our exercises," he repeated over and over as his fingers traced out the same pattern in the air. Over and over again he repeated the rhyme, oblivious to the dust, and to the constant buzzing. As his fingers moved he marveled at them. He marveled at the perfect symmetry of their movements. They seemed to move without thought. He tested this idea by thinking of another song at the same time the fingers beat out the rhyme. His fingers never missed a beat, but continued to move. As the fly's buzzing grew fainter and stopped, and the last grains of dust settled on his hands, he looked up at the light and smiled. "Ashes to ashes, dust to dust," he said. "How appropriate."

The exercises had kept a certain thought from his mind, a thought that now was finding its way into his consciousness. "I have to exercise so I can feed it when it's hungry, but they won't let me feed it," he burst out, his irritated voice filling the room. It's hungry, he thought. It's all ready to eat, but they're not going to let me feed it. Now it's unhappy, but not as unhappy as I am—I'm terribly unhappy, and it's hungry! He drew in a deep breath and leaned back looking at the light. A frown crossed his face. Get a grip on yourself, he thought. You're beginning to like feeding it more than it likes to eat. It's a job, like this one! When they tell you it's time to feed it, then you feed it. Otherwise, leave it alone. He shifted his position in the chair. Hell, I can feed it when I want, and it's hungry. Does it matter that I like feeding it? It's no crime to like beauty! It's no crime to bring beauty into the world! He shifted his gaze toward his fingers. No, I can't let the feeding control me! It's dangerous, too dangerous!

Now he watched him come closer, carefully measuring the distance. Come closer, he thought. Come a little closer, that's it—now! Then he watched him move away, and the jaws opened too late. I had to let him go, they said so! But he was old. What old man wouldn't like to bring beauty into this world at the moment he leaves it? What's he good for anyway? This might have been the highlight of his life. I should have fed it anyway! I don't care what they say next time. Now I might have to feed it someone else!

"Dangerous thoughts," he said out loud, "dangerous thoughts." I'll get out, he thought. That will show them. Let them find another. Twisting in his chair, he focused back to his hands. So beautiful, and slender, he thought, they need a few more times of grace. What's the harm in waiting a while longer? They said I might get to feed it soon if things didn't work out—glad I don't know what things—glad I don't know anything about them—glad for my beautiful hands—glad I love beauty—so—I'll stay and feed it a few more times, then leave it to feed itself.

CHAPTER NINE

EIGHT DOWN

S EVEN WEEKS HAD PASSED since Karen had first lucid dreamed together with Stephen. The first Saturday night after that first time, Karen had gone to bed determined not to lucid dream. However, sleep has a way of dampening reservations. So that night and all the other early Sunday mornings after, Karen met Stephen, always on the same bench, and each time she experienced the feeling of being two Karens—one Karen safely in bed, the other beside Stephen. Each time, as they rose from the bench, she blended into one. Each time, they walked into a different world, every one unique, but each one as beautiful as the next. For Karen it was wonderful. In the dreams she felt attractive and desirable. In the dreams she wanted Stephen to look at her, to want her as much as the Sun and Wind did. Every dream ended with her whole body swept into the air, sensations too strong to sustain pulsing through her body. Every dream ended with Karen soaked with sweat, bolting out of her dream into her bed. Stephen told her it was possible to not wake, but to follow the sensations through; not to be afraid, but to follow them to the end. Stephen told Karen that if she could learn to not wake, he could teach her something even more amazing and satisfying.

LUCID DREAMS

Between Sundays, Karen and Stephen never spoke of the lucid dreams. Sometimes Stephen would ask Karen why she looked so tired on Monday, but she never took the bait, and Stephen never acted as if he questioned the excuses she gave him. She was beginning to really enjoy her work. Stephen had taught her to analyze surface weather maps. The computer plotted out the information on a map, and could even draw lines of equal pressure and temperature on it. However, Stephen was emphatic that a computer, however capable, was not up to the actual analysis. Instead he taught her the old skill of hand analysis, as it had been done years ago, before computers did most of the work. Karen seemed to have a knack for that type of hand work. After several weeks of work her weather maps were drawn accurately. She liked working with Stephen. He hadn't tried to push himself on her in any way, and she was starting to feel comfortable around him. Gary hadn't mentioned anything further to her about their suspicions concerning Jim Fulton's disappearance, or any connection to the odd scrambled station reports. In fact, the last couple of weeks, Karen had forgotten all about her brief stint as a sleuth.

"Well, Karen," Stephen said, leaning over her shoulder and looking at her map, "I'm proud of you. That map you're working on is turning out very well. Anyone would be proud to draw a map as nice as that one. Most old time meteorologists would be hard pressed to do as well, but I'm not sure what they would think of a woman doing this work."

"Do you really think so?" Karen replied, glancing at Stephen. "I've been trying hard to improve my skills. About those old meteorologists, I think they would like the fact that I'm carrying on their traditions."

"I suppose you're right, but some men wouldn't care if you were the best in the world. They just wouldn't want any woman doing what they think should be done by a man. Anyway, what you're doing looks all right to me."

Stephen moved around Karen, and picked up the map. He looked at it for several minutes, lost in his own thoughts. "What are you thinking," queried Karen. "Is there something about the map you don't like? Can I improve it in some way?"

"This map is almost perfect, from a scientific point of view," Stephen remarked as he turned to look at her. "It's even better than it needs to be for most purposes. We can use this map for any studies we need it for and it will be fine. However, there's more to life than pure utility. Sometimes we create things only for their beauty, and we don't care whether what we create is useful beyond that. Here, you've created a map that has tremendous utility. Would you like to go further and make this map into something beautiful for its own sake? I wouldn't ask you if I didn't feel you could do it. By going for beauty, the science can be even better."

"How can that be true?" Karen injected. "It doesn't seem right that concentrating on the beauty of the map would improve the science in it. The way I draw now, I concentrate on being accurate to the numbers on the map, and making as scientifically correct a rendering as possible."

"Sometimes the harder we try to reach perfection in something, the further it slips away. Here, try this. Try drawing this map again, but try drawing not for scientific accuracy. Try to make the lines fit together in a smooth pattern, a pattern that is beautiful to look at. Try to draw contours that flow together, lose yourself in your drawing, forget about science, work only for the beauty you can bring. Think of something other than your work. Here—give it a try," Stephen said as he handed the map back to Karen. "You would be surprised what can be beautiful if one works for beauty. Even the grotesque can be beautiful. Yes, even the grotesque."

"Well, I'll try, but I'm not too hopeful," Karen replied, taking the map and laying it down on the desk. "I'll start right after lunch."

It was a beautiful day and Karen left the confines of the building to enjoy her lunch hour in her favorite spot on the campus. She made her way down to the small clearing guarded by the wooden monkeys. She sat down on the grass next to the post that one of the monkeys sat on. Looking up at the monkey she asked, "Oh sir, what am I to make of Stephen? At first I thought he would be like other middle-aged men I've known—you know—trying to find some type of line to use on me. But now I don't know, I just don't know. He's brought me into his private world, and he could have had me in his dream—our dream, but he hasn't. OK, OK, you're right. He's given me the best climaxes of my life, so strong I can't even sustain them, and have to draw back. What's that? You're right. It's not enough. I need something more. Sure, I like being naked in front of him, but why won't he touch me? Do I want him to? Yes, in my dreams I do—I'm not so sure about it when I'm not dreaming. I wish I knew how I should feel. And now he wants me to draw maps for beauty, but he says he's satisfied with my work as it is. And this talk of beauty and the grotesque—every time I think I'm starting to understand him just a little, he does something to change my mind. Hey, are you still listening to me? Well, if you won't, I'll try the fish in the pond."

Karen rose to her feet, turning her back to the monkeys. Without bowing as she normally did, she moved over to sit on the ledge of the small brick-edged pond. "Tell me," she said looking down at the fish in the shadows of the overhanging leaves, "does having your brains in water all the time make you smarter than those monkeys? It does? Good. Maybe you can help me to understand how I'm supposed to feel. How can someone have the best sex ever and not be satisfied? What? Then it's not the best sex ever? You're no better help than the monkeys." Karen stood up and turned to leave. As she passed the monkeys she stopped suddenly and turned. "What's that? The midday sun makes everything appear as it really is? If I don't want to hear the truth come back in the evening sun? And what? Don't wake up this Sunday, and don't be afraid? Hey, I'm not afraid. Thanks for the advice, guys. See ya later, time to get back to work."

As Karen stepped out of the elevator into the hallway, a buzz of voices filled her ears. Clumps of students stood around talking in excited voices.

"Hey, Karen!" Janet called, as she leaned out of her office door, "what's a six letter word for sex type?

"Karen!" Stephen called from down the hall, "could I see you a minute?"

Just as Karen turned to answer Janet, Gary accosted her. "You and I need to talk", he said breaking away from a group of anxious students who had gathered around him.

Noticing that Stephen was still in the hallway waiting outside his door, Karen hurried down the hallway toward his room. On the way, she noticed several students working on what looked like a crossword puzzle. When she reached Stephen, he moved inside motioning her to follow. Closing the door behind her, Stephen sat down.

"What's all the excitement?" Karen asked, moving to stand across from Stephen "Was there a break-in?"

"Something like that," Stephen replied. "The computer system was broken into over the lunch hour. Preliminary checks indicate that nothing was damaged, but Gary will have to complete more in-depth testing before we'll know for sure. Check all your files carefully, and you'll have to change your password as soon as possible. That's about it except I suspect everyone will spend some time working the puzzle. Go ahead and work it and get it out of the way. Then get back to work."

"What puzzle?" Karen quizzed. "You mean the one Janet asked me about, and people are working on in the hallway?"

"That's the one," Stephen said getting up and walking Karen to the door. Ushering her out of the room, Stephen glanced up and down the hallway.

"Looking for someone?" Karen asked.

"No," Stephen remarked, quickly moving back into the room, "just seeing if the commotion has died down."

As soon as Karen stepped back into the hallway, Janet leaned back into the hallway. "Have you thought of a six letter word for sex type yet?" Karen answered with a puzzled look. Seeing her confusion, Janet invited Karen into her office. "Here, we can work it together. Let's see if we can work it before Gary can. We could try beating Stephen, but knowing him, I don't think he'll work it."

"What are you working on?" Karen asked as she sat down beside Janet at her desk.

Janet picked up one of a group of well-sharpened pencils lying neatly in a row and pointed to a crossword puzzle on her desk. "That's it," she said. "Whoever broke into the computer system left a crossword puzzle in everyone's home directory. All you have to do is print it out. It's called 'cwrdpuz'. But why bother? There won't be any reason to after we finish."

"OK, let's do it. The word you want is 'gender,'" Karen offered.

"That's right. I was thinking of another word for sex, not male or female."

"What's the next word you need?"

"Seven down is a seven letter word for a young wild bird. It starts with an "f" and ends with an "r". That's a hard one."

EIGHT DOWN

"Check in the almanac, a page or two after the weather records," Karen said. " I saw a listing of the names for young animals when I was looking up the world's record rainfall, which is twelve inches in forty two minutes in 1947 at Holt, Missouri, if you're curious."

"Here it is," Janet replied, reaching onto a shelf over her desk. "I'll work on the next word while you're looking it up."

Karen quickly thumbed through the pages. "They're called flappers!"

"The next word is the inventor of the steam-powered boat. That's easy. I learned about him in the sixth grade. His last name is Fulton, and look, it fits right in the spot."

After an hour of hard work, Karen and Janet had almost finished the crossword puzzle. "One word to go," sighed Janet. "This puzzle was harder that I thought it would be, but it looks like Gary is still working on it."

Karen read the last clue. "First name of the two-word name for the laws which governed the behavior of blacks in the old south. Hmmmm. That would be Jim Crow." As Karen reached over and wrote in the last word, she suddenly froze. Together in the third row was the name Jim Fulton.

"What's the matter Karen?" Janet asked. "You seem startled."

"Look at the third row! It's the name of the missing student, Jim Fulton."

"Oh, is that all? He's not missing, just run off. And what would his name be doing on this puzzle anyway? Hey! Maybe he's the one who broke into the system. I would think he would be smarter than to leave his name as evidence."

Karen tried to sound calmer as she answered Janet. "I suppose you're right. I was just startled to see his name, that's all. Well, Gary wants to see me. Do you mind if I take a copy of the puzzle so I can rub it in to Gary that we solved it already?"

"Sure, but don't make a copy. I don't need to keep this original. Have fun rubbing it in."

Karen hurried across to Gary's room. As he turned to face her, he held up a copy of the puzzle and mouthed the words. "We really need to talk." Turning toward the hallway, and in a slightly louder than normal voice, Gary announced. "I'll talk to you later, Karen. I just have a few details to go over concerning the changing of your password. Now I have an errand to run, and I'll be back in about an hour. See you then, back at my room." As Gary stood up he silently pointed to a map of the campus. A light circle was drawn around the marshland across from the athletic fields. Without further words, Gary turned and quickly walked out.

CHAPTER 10

MARSHLAND

How the marshland came into being is an interesting story. The university was built next to a large lake which now was mostly an urban lake with one notable exception. Long before environmental laws were even thought of, the city used the wide reach of land between the eastern edge of the University and the lake shore to deposit garbage. Tons and tons of garbage were dumped, first away from the lake, then, as the pile increased, right up to the lake shore. Seagulls found the dump irresistible and congregated there in great numbers in the mornings. On nice days, when the afternoon sun would cause large bubbles of air to rise aloft from the hot walkways and roofs of the University, groups of seagulls would take off from the dump and float on the hot, rising air. As the seagulls spiraled overhead, hapless students would run for cover. Eventually, the mess was too much even for the most ardent opponent of government regulations. Laws were passed to protect the city's shorelines. The dumping was moved elsewhere, the garbage was leveled, and tons and tons of dirt were used to cover the stench. Parking lots were built on some of the fill, but a large part was deemed unfit to build on and left to return to its natural state. As time moved on, a strange thing began to happen—sort of an added bonus that no one had predicted. As the garbage began to settle under the fill dirt, patches of ground started settling at vastly different rates. The outcome was a lake shore composed of a wide variety of habitats. Marshy pools alternate with hillocks of bushes and trees. Tall grasses are interspersed with small meadows of flowers. The result is God's little acre for birds and bird watchers. So much of the city was overrun by a true scavenger, the crow, that even in winter, people often came to enjoy the lake shore and observe the large variety of birds not seen anymore in the neighborhoods.

Karen didn't know any of this history as she slipped out of the building on the pretext of going to the library, and made her way through the last of the campus and on towards the lake shore. If she would have bothered to have asked Stephen, he could have told her the whole story, one with a novel twist. He could have told her that when he was a student, his old professor would take them out in the afternoon to watch the seagulls turning around and around overhead.

"Perfect, just perfect," the old man would say. "A fine example of relative motion. The seagulls glide downward, the air rises upward, and the clever birds rotate around and around, never losing altitude." By the time Stephen became a professor, the seagulls had long gone to better feeding areas. Not even the prospects of riding the currents and watching the students scatter could bring them back.

Karen passed the entrance sign and started up the first path. People were gathered in small groups, looking through binoculars and pointing at trees and bushes. At first Karen didn't notice Gary standing by himself toward the lake shore. Short paths ran toward the shore from the main path, some ending on platforms that hung over the water. Lovers often claimed the more secluded ones, but the weather was somewhat cold for summer, so Gary had managed to find an empty one.

"This one isn't very hidden, but it will have to do," Gary said, as he buttoned up his sweater. "Maybe this cold day will keep people away from here."

"You saw it?" Karen asked, pulling her own sweater closer to her.

"I sure did," exclaimed Gary, "and I was just about to give up on this whole business of coded messages and code breaking."

"What do you mean?"

"I've been running the code breaking program for weeks, with nothing to show for my work. Hours and hours of computer time for nothing, absolutely nothing. I'd begun to feel that we were jumping to conclusions—you know, the bit about Fulton's disappearance. Last week the new computer we ordered finally arrived. I don't like to hook a new computer directly up to the network right away, there might be bugs in the operating system, or other problems that I can't foresee. Anyway, I always run them for sort of a shake down time, then hook them up to the Net. This computer is ten times faster than the ones we have. Looking around for some program to try, I decided to run the decoding program on it—just as a test—since I'd lost interest in breaking the code. It was a good test program since it used large amounts of memory. So, I transferred all the files containing the scrambled station reports and the code breaking program to the new computer and started it running. Then I did something that might, just might, keep us alive."

"Keep us alive?" gasped Karen. "What do you mean, keep us alive?"

"I always clean out my trace back files when I finish with a job,"

Gary replied, pushing his hair back from his forehead with his hand.

"Trace back files?"

"Yes, trace back files. Every time a command is typed into a keyboard the line is saved in a special file called a trace back file. The files are hidden so they won't clutter up the directories. They are mostly text, so they take up little space. If some problem occurs, the trace back files are a handy way of figuring out what might have happened. Sometimes programmers write selected outputs to the trace back files to help in tracing how a long-running program is progressing. Unless something goes wrong, most people forget about them. That's why I clean them out when a job is done. It's a good time to remember they are there, and start with a clean file for the next job."

"How did that keep us alive?"

Gary lowered his voice as two people passed offshore in a canoe. "The break-in to the computer system tipped me off. At first I thought it was just some prank by hackers. Especially when the crossword puzzle was left in everyone's home directory. It's an old trick of hackers—to leave something behind as a calling card —sort of to say, 'Hey, look at me, look at how smart I am!' and the puzzle was nice and clever. I started to work it like everyone else, and then I saw his name, you know, Jim Fulton."

"Yeah, Janet and I saw it too, but Janet laughed it off as a weird coincidence. She even suggested that Jim might be the hacker who broke in," Karen interjected.

"Ha," scoffed Gary. "Jim couldn't hack his way into his own computer, let alone our system. Actually, at first I wasn't alarmed. Then, during a check of what files the hackers might have interfered with, I noticed an odd pattern by accident. I decided to check my trace back files on a whim. Normally, there wouldn't be a way to check if anyone has accessed a trace back file, but I've written a program to keep check on how much they're used."

"Why would you do that?" queried Karen, wondering whether Gary thought like normal people.

"Oh—just one of my hobbies—," Gary replied, looking away from Karen. "I looked at my trace back file and noticed that it had been copied out over the Net, to an unknown address. I quickly checked all the other trace back files and every one had been copied also."

"What's so odd about that?" asked Karen, beginning to feel calmer about the whole break-in.

"Don't you see!" Gary asked, raising his voice. "The trace back files are good for only two things, to help trace problems, or as a record of all commands typed in the computer. Someone who knows programming can reconstruct everything that went on in our small system. That's the point—it's a small system with relatively slow computers. No hacker smart enough to break into our system would want it for anything—so why be interested in our activities? Then it struck me, they must have been looking for evidence—evidence that someone was interested in the scrambled files. Thank heavens I moved the code breaking program onto the new computer! Since the new computer was off the Net they couldn't know about it, and deleting the trace back file erased any trace of our activities on the other computers."

"But, but why is Jim Fulton's name in the crossword?" Karen stammered. "Why give us an obvious hint, and possibly give away the purpose of the break in?"

"Ego. All great crime figures have it, and sometimes their ego leads to their downfall. Some clever people can't stand it that no one will ever know that they committed the perfect crime. It gnaws and gnaws at them until they brag to someone, or leave clues for the police. I only know of one master crook that didn't brag. Cooper, J. B. Cooper. He extorted millions, then bailed out of a passenger jet over wilderness and was never heard from again. He either kept his mouth shut or ended up bear bait. But, whoever broke in to our computer can't help bragging about it, showing off that he got rid of Fulton, and leaving clues to show us how smart he is."

"This is so hard to believe. Who would do this, and why the puzzle?"

"To make it look like a simple hacker joke. To cover up the real purpose."

"What can we do?" blurted out Karen. "What's our next move?"

"Well, I'm sure that the hackers, or maybe they're even killers, left a program somewhere on our disks that will alert them if anyone does anything suspicious with the scrambled files."

"What would be suspicious?" asked Karen.

"I don't think that simply deleting the scrambled files would make them suspicious. But, if we collect them all together in one file, or move them somewhere — that might. So, I'm thinking, maybe we should just ignore the scrambled files, or better yet, let's delete them as they come in. If someone is really monitoring our moves — let's play it cool. Let's not give them any excuse to move against us," ventured Gary.

"Can you find the program and delete it?"

"I could, but then they'd know we know. Better to let them think that we don't know about it."

"But, how will we break the code if we can't collect the odd reports?"

"The National Weather Service collects the same data. If we're desperate for more information, we can hang out there and collect some."

"That would be really hard to do," Karen interjected. "We couldn't collect the data on a computer. We'd have to write it down. Combing through all the data to look for the odd reports—it'd take hours. I don't think that's feasible."

"OK. I think you're right, but we can go every week to make a spot check—just to see if the odd reports are still coming through on the data Net from the National Weather Service."

"Yeah—that's a good idea. If they stop sending, then they might be on to us and afraid to send any code! We can use it as sort of a trip wire. It's not much of a trip wire, but it's all we have. But, what about the code? Can we break it?"

"I don't really know," Gary answered. As of a week ago, I hadn't had any luck at all. But that was before I started running on the new, faster computer. Unfortunately, that's over tomorrow."

"Over tomorrow? Why tomorrow?" asked Karen with increasing curiosity.

"Tomorrow, Stephen wants me to hook it up to our system. I've already put him off a couple of days. I can't delay him much longer. I promised him tomorrow would be the day."

"I could talk to him. Tell him our ideas and get him to delay the installation for a few days more," offered Karen.

"You can if you want, but I wouldn't even consider it. How can I tell him I've been using his new computer to track down some potential killers? I'd look stupid, especially since we don't have any real evidence, just wild guesses."

Karen turned a light shade of red. "I guess you're right. I'd sound pretty silly, and he might be mad that I've been wasting work time. So, what are our choices? Do we have any?"

"Let's go back up. Come back to my room. While I'm changing your password, we can look at the latest results from the code breaking program. We might have gotten lucky."

Gary started to leave, but stopped mid-turn. A small man was standing right behind them. Startled, Karen bumped into Gary, then looked at the man. He was holding a limp bird in his hand. Karen started to apologize for hitting Gary, but the man broke in.

"I'm sorry to have surprised you. I was walking down the main path when I noticed this bird lying beneath this bush. I bent down to see if it was dead. I didn't even notice you until you turned. You actually gave me quite a scare."

"It was our fault!" Gary managed to say, regaining his composure. "What kind of a bird is it?"

The man held the bird gently in his hands, cradling its still head in his fingers. "Death—it can be beautiful. See how still it lays? How the wings spread out from the body? See the curve of the line of its neck? Death hasn't dimmed its colors." He held the bird out to Karen, but Karen drew back behind Gary.

"Don't be afraid of death," he said to Karen. "Look for the beauty in it. Here, hold it."

As he held out his hands, Karen noticed how long and slender his fingers were and a chill ran up the back of her neck. "I'm sorry. I—I can't. It's silly, but when I was a child I was told never to touch anything dead. Could you excuse us? We're really late to work," Karen said as she edged past him and quickly moved onto the main path. Gary stammered out some additional excuse and hurried after Karen.

"Whoa—who was that?" asked Karen.

"Whoa—you can repeat that for me—he sure startled me!" Gary replied, glancing back over his shoulder. He was relieved to see that the stranger was still standing by the water holding the dead bird, not looking after them at all. "Did you see the length of his fingers?" Gary remarked to Karen. "I've never seen such long and delicate fingers."

"I haven't either," Karen said. "Do you think he's a surgeon? That might explain why he's not afraid of death."

"I don't think so. I can see him bending over a dead body, those slender fingers draining out all the blood. He must be an undertaker. That's my guess."

"He's not big enough to lift a body—he might be a—"

"A creep," Gary interrupted. "Maybe they let him play with the bodies as payment for draining them."

After Gary spoke, they increased their pace as they hurried up from the marshland. Neither spoke until they approached their building. "You'd better go in without me," Gary said. "I'll come up the back stairs and meet you in a couple of minutes. I don't want anyone in our building to see us together."

"Here's the output," Gary said when they met several minutes later. He glanced out into the hall checking to see if anyone was close. "Let's look at it. It looks like something might be here."

All Karen saw was a long list of numbers and letters on the page. "What does all this mean?" she asked.

"The program is first listing all the letter or number combinations that occur more than once. Most occur two times, but a few have occurred more often. Here's one that is interesting. It's occurred over fifty times in the more than a thousand lines of station reports." Karen looked at the combination of letters. There were three letters in a row—BCG.

"Is that a word?" she asked. "It doesn't mean anything to me."

"No, it's not a word as it reads. It's in code. Look here, the program has succeeded in isolating the first letter. See it's B_ _. The program suggests it's a three letter word starting with B, but it hasn't been able to decipher the other two letters."

"How can it do that?"

"Code breaking programs look for combinations that reoccur

and then guess at a meaning for the combination. After that the programs check to see if a guess makes any sense in combination with other guesses. It's complicated, but believe me, they work. They just take time to run—time we don't have!"

"This is a wild guess, but suppose, since this is a weather message, the three letters stand for a station name," Karen suggested. "It might have been left in accidentally when they coded up the message, by mistake or something."

"Anyone smart enough to put out a code this difficult to break, and able enough to use the weather data distribution network to send it out, won't make mistakes," Gary retorted.

"Well—they certainty made a mistake if they left a clue in the crossword puzzle!" Karen shot back. "Check out my idea, just to humor me."

Gary shrugged, turned to his terminal and typed a command that brought up the three letter code for each station, along with the name, the latitude, longitude, and the elevation. He scrolled down the page until he reached the codes starting with B. Karen began to read them out loud at random. "BKE-Baker, Oregon; BKF-Denver, Colorado; BIS—Bismarck, North Dakota; BGS-Big Springs, Texas; BKH-Kekaha, Hawaii; BTM-Butte, Montana. Gads! There must be over a hundred!"

"There are slightly under a hundred. But, that's only the stations in the U.S. What about the stations in the rest of the world?" Gary asked. "There are probably over a thousand that would start with a B. Do you want to bring those up on the screen too?"

"No, my idea is way off base—forget it. Is there any other information in the printout that can tell us anything?"

Gary turned away from the screen to stare at the pages of printout. "Look, there's another combination that's used lots of times also. It's OR57G9."

"Does the program have a guess at what it is?" Karen queried. "Look! The program has suggested several choices. 'Orphan girl, spoon rack, swoon pack, point'—what does this mean?"

"It means we've struck out!" Gary replied, folding up the print-out and throwing it in the recycling. "Even if one of these words is right, how can we put anything together with these choices? No chance! Let's work on your password."

When Karen stood up to leave, she paused to ask one final question in a low voice. "Do you think this is all in our heads? Are we following real leads or are we putting together a string of coincidences? After all, what do we really have? A student walks out; he's intrigued with a set of scrambled station reports; someone breaks into our system; they leave a puzzle in everyone's home directory; two words in the puzzle spell the name of the missing student; they might or might not have left a program to snoop on us; we can't check for fear we'll be caught; we get nowhere with breaking the code, if there really is one to break. So, what does it all add up to? Nothing, that's what! See you tomorrow, I'm going home."

As Karen turned to walk out into the hall Gary looked at her and shrugged, then turned back to his programming.

CHAPTER ELEVEN

DON'T BE AFRAID

"DON'T BE AFRAID, don't be afraid, don't be afraid, don't be afraid," Karen repeated to herself. "What was it that Stephen said? Follow it through to the end, then he could teach me. Teach me what?" But, by now Karen couldn't focus on what Stephen meant. The wind was beginning to circle her legs, the sun was burning hot on her breasts.

"Don't be afraid, don't be afraid, don't be afraid," she whispered.

The wind was more aggressive now. It stroked her legs with increasing strength. The sun released its grip on her breasts. Karen began to shake uncontrollably.

"Don't be afraid, don't be afraid, don't be afraid," she whispered.

The sun hadn't returned, but the wind had swept her off the ground. Karen tried to control her shaking, but couldn't. The wind was supporting her in the small of her back. Her hair hung down away from her body. Karen was weak with anticipation.

"Don't be afraid, don't be afraid, don't be afraid," she whispered.

She felt the sun return to the soles of her feet. It slowly moved around, then up her ankles.

"Don't be afraid, don't be afraid, don't be afraid," she whispered.

The wind lifted her higher and moved her towards the warmth of the sun. The sun caressed the insides of her calves, then the wind swirled around her, lifting her legs.

"Don't be afraid, don't be afraid, don't be afraid," she whispered.

The sun moved along the inside of her thighs. It stroked her skin, each stroke moving ever so slightly higher. Then a gust of wind caught her.

"Don't be afraid, don't be afraid, don't be afraid," she whispered.

The sun stopped moving up her legs for a moment as Karen lay in the air, shaking. Waves of trembling moved through her. Her breaths were deep and pulsing. She saw the wooden monkeys standing beside her, like flanking guards.

"Don't be afraid, don't be afraid, don't be afraid," she whispered.

The left monkey called out to the wind. "Now."

The right monkey called out to the sun. "Now."

"Don't be afraid, don't be afra------"

The wind gripped her with a strong hand. The hard hot rays of the sun penetrated deep inside her.

"Push, Karen, push into the warmth," the left monkey urged.

"Bear down, Karen, bear down, follow the warmth," the right monkey coached.

Karen pushed into the beams. Feelings of rapture surged through her body. Karen heard moans, like some wild animal in torment. They were coming from deep within her. She tried to stop them, but the moans increased with each new surge of warmth. The monkeys called to her on the wind. "Bear down, give birth, don't be afraid!"

Karen pushed against the warmth with all her strength. Suddenly she felt in control. She pushed harder into the warmth. Spasms of pleasure filled her. Karen arched her head back with the effort. She pushed hard as the pulses of warmth pushed inside. With one final effort she bore down with incredible strength. She felt the warmth pass out of her body. During what seemed like forever, it flowed and flowed, taking with it her strength. The wind relaxed its strong hands and cradled her body with soft fingers. A light warm rain began to fall on her, washing away any scent of the sun. A warm wind blew over her, not stroking, but embracing her in its warmth. It dried and warmed her, soothing her tired muscles. Suddenly Karen was overcome with the urge to sleep. She closed her eyes as the wind gently laid her back in the bed of flowers.

Karen lazily stretched out her whole body, feeling the smoothness of the sheets of her own bed on her bare legs. She felt wonderful. I'm so relaxed, she thought. "What's that lovely scent?" she asked out loud to no one. "Why, it's me! I smell like the bed of flowers I laid in." Without showering, and even though it was Sunday, Karen dressed and hurried to the university. She ran down the familiar paths into the small glen guarded by the wooden monkeys.

"Smell me, smell me!" Karen called as she whirled past them, dancing onto the grass. "That scent? It's the scent of the bed, the bed that the wind and the sun made only for me. For me. I love who I am! I'm the mistress of the wind and the sun! Oh, it's lovely. I'm the one they want." Karen whirled over to the pond, and looked at her reflection in the still water. For the first time outside of her dreams she felt pretty and attractive. Karen brushed her hair back from her face and admired her features. "I always thought I was plain," she spoke to the goldfish in the shadows as her fingers chased them from their hiding places. "But, if I'm plain, it's a plainness loved by the earth, and the wind, and the sun. After all, much of nature is plain, but nature loves her own." Karen spent the morning lying on the grass, looking at the blue sky filled with small white clouds, and thinking how perfectly, perfectly wonderful life was.

When Karen arrived for work Monday morning, she still hadn't lost all the feelings from her lucid dream. As she passed by Janet's office, Janet came out into the hallway. "What's that perfume you're wearing, Karen? It smells fresh, like the scent of wildflowers on the wind."

"Oh, its a new bath salt I'm trying out, called Sun and Wind." Karen called back to her as she brushed past.

"Wait a minute, Karen," Janet implored. "Where can I get some?"

"Don't know," Karen replied, thinking fast on her feet. "Someone was giving out samples on the street."

"Did you save the container? It might list the maker."

"Sorry. I threw it away, and garbage pickup at my place is Monday morning."

Janet reluctantly returned to her office. "Those bath salts must be something new. Karen's skin looks radiant and the smell is just lovely," Janet remarked to herself.

Karen looked in at Stephen as he was working, bent over his desk. "Well?" she asked as he looked up. Stephen didn't say anything for a few moments, but simply looked at her. Slowly he took in her scent and he knew what the ending of her dream was. They never before had spoken of the lucid dreams, and he was at a loss for words. Stephen desperately wanted to admit how he felt about her, today, but words seemed to stick in his throat since neither of them had acknowledged the dreams to the other.

"You--you," he started to say, but Karen interrupted him.

"Well," she said with a boldness unusual for her. "Now, how about teaching me about things you said were even more amazing than I could imagine."

Karen had never seen Stephen look so disconcerted. "I -- I -- I will, but not here—not next time, but when you're ready, then I will teach you," he managed to say, trying to speak in a normal voice.

"What do you think of my new bath salts?" Karen asked as she moved closer to his desk, putting out her arm for him to smell.

"Nice," Stephen said, trying to appear calm. "Very nice."

"Don't you want to get closer and enjoy its subtle nuances?" Karen asked, surprised at her sudden boldness.

"No," Stephen replied, motioning for her to let him get back to work. "Can you come back later? We have some things to go over I've noticed in your last week's work. What about after lunch? I won't be so busy then."

Karen, sensing his reluctance to personalize their relationship outside of the dreams, replied to Stephen in as business-like a tone as possible. "Sure, that'd be fine with me. I'll be back after lunch. I'll see you then."

After Karen had left his office, Stephen buried his head in his hands. "Why? Why couldn't I tell her how good she smelled," he thought. "What's the matter with me? Why couldn't I tell her how much I want her? Will I never be able to love a woman again like other men?" Raising his head, Stephen turned back to his desk, hoping to lose his anguish in his work.

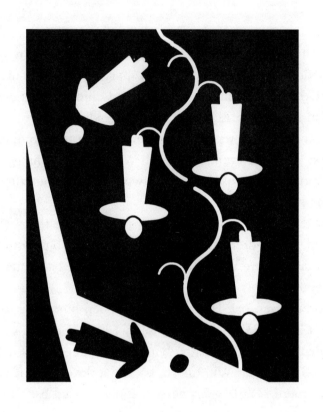

CHAPTER TWELVE

ELK LODGE

"How is it that Karen smells so good every Monday?" Janet asked Gary. "I thought she only had a sample of the bath salts. I can't believe that she could still have any left."

"I've noticed it, too," Gary replied. "Some of the students are making remarks as well. It's kind of funny. Some students really like her scent. Others, not so much."

"How do you feel about it?"

"I like it. It reminds me of a smell from childhood."

"From childhood?"

"My uncle owned a farm out by the coast. We stayed a couple of weeks in the summer, my sister and I. There was a meadow surrounded by tall trees that we liked to play in. My sister and I would go there to play early in the morning, before the dampness was gone. In late summer the meadow was full of small flowers. I don't know what they were, but when they first opened, and the meadow was still damp, the scent was like Karen's. Fresh and clean, and earthy. When she walks by me on Mondays, the scent takes me back to those times."

"My, Gary, you're sounding like an advertisement for those bath salts, or whatever they are."

"Well, if I had a woman, my first gift to her would be a package of those, whatever they are," Gary remarked as he drifted out the door.

"Hmmm," Janet thought. "What's with Gary? I've never heard him even mention a woman, any woman. I wonder...?"

Just then Karen walked by Janet's door. "Hey, Karen," Janet called. "Stephen would like to see you."

"What's it about?"

"You'll see."

Stephen was looking out the window when Karen came into his office. Karen didn't say anything for a few minutes, but she stood quietly, watching Stephen. Karen's feelings had changed since she had first met him. He hadn't tried to come on to her in any way at work. He was kind and fair, and he never seemed to raise his voice, at least not when she was around. Karen wasn't sure of his looks when she first met him, but now she rather liked how he looked. In fact, she was beginning to really like him. However, she had trouble reconciling the Stephen who was her boss at work and the Stephen who was her guide in their dreams. As Karen stood watching him, she felt like slipping out of her clothes and asking him, "Do you recognize me? I'm the woman in your dreams." The urge to confront him became so strong that she purposely knocked some papers from his desk, just to stop her thoughts.

"Karen!" Stephen said, as he turned towards her. "You're just the person I wanted to see. Do you see the tops of those clouds?"

Karen bent forward to look. "Do you mean those low ones by the tower?"

"Yes, look at the tops of the ones to the right of the tower. Do you see the curls of cloud at the top? They're breaking waves, like when the ocean waves break on the shore. See how they curl?"

"Some look like jelly rolls," Karen noted. "What makes them?"

"Wind shear. The wind is blowing faster the higher above the cloud top you go. I don't mean the higher you go specifically, but if you were there you would notice an increase of the wind with height. There are more requirements, like stability, and other things. Given the right combination of things, those waves happen."

"Thanks for the explanation. Whatever the reason, they sure are beautiful. Janet said you wanted to see me?"

"Yes. I'm having a small gathering at my house this Saturday. It will start right after lunch. We'll have dinner about five. That will make it so that you can get to bed early, if you want to. I'm also inviting Gary and Janet. Gary was nice enough to offer Janet a ride. You can ride with them if you like, or bring your own car. Here's a map," Stephen said, as he picked up a piece of paper from the many piles on his desk. "It's about an hour from the University."

Karen studied the map carefully. "Is there any difference between taking the route that goes out the Tidal Basin Road and the one that uses Sunset Highway?" she asked.

"Not really. The time is about the same. The Tidal Basin Road is more scenic, but sometimes the draw bridge over the river goes up. If I'm in a hurry, I don't take that route. If you come that way, you will need to first come over the floating bridge that's east of the university. During traffic times, that bridge can be real crowded. Would you like a recommendation?"

"Sure."

"Take the Tidal Basin Road route coming out. It will be Saturday and the traffic won't be bad. Come back on Sunset Highway.

It might be dark and Tidal Basin Road doesn't have any houses along it for quite a ways. I guess if you had car trouble, you could walk to the bridge tender. That could be pretty far in the dark, though, and I think the tender might go home before midnight."

"OK, I'll think about your recommendation," Karen replied, moving towards the door.

"Does this mean you'll come?" Stephen asked, trying not to seem too anxious.

"It sounds like fun. Can I bring anything?"

"No. Just bring yourself. My kids are looking forward to meeting you. We'll see you there."

Karen enjoyed the drive out to Stephen's house on Saturday. The traffic on the floating bridge was light and once over the bridge, the city gave way to suburbs, then to scattered houses. Tidal Basin Road was winding, but well traveled during the day. East of the bridge, the road straightened out, and began to pass by small farms, populated by mostly horses and a few beef cows. Stephen's map was easy to follow, and Karen was pleased to find she had arrived on time. Turning the last corner, she came upon what seemed like two large log homes, linked together by a small walkway. The yard wasn't large compared to the small farms that Karen had just passed, but the grass was neatly cut. What looked like an orchard stood behind the second house. Karen noticed a small garden in the front containing a few flowers, but mostly covered with pumpkin vines and corn stalks. Just as Karen was about to get out of the car, Gary and Janet drove up behind her.

"Hi, Karen," Janet said, opening the passenger side of Gary's car. "Wow! What a big house. Is it two houses or all one? Let's go inside and see."

"Haven't you been here before?" Karen remarked to Janet.

"No, and Gary hasn't either. I'm so excited at finally getting a chance to see the house he built! Look, the wooden sign over the door says Elk Lodge. What a strange name for a house. I wonder what it means?"

Beating the others up to the door, Janet searched for the door-bell. Having no luck in locating it, Janet finally knocked. "Hello," she called as she knocked. "Anybody home?"

Excited voices came running towards the door from the other side.

"Hey, let me answer it," Jill cried.

"Let me go! I was here first," yelled Andy.

"You're too young!"

"Dad wanted me to do it!"

"Shush—they'll hear you," complained Jill.

Suddenly the door flew open and there stood two well-scrubbed children. The girl looked like a teenager, and the boy was younger.

"Hi," Janet said, stepping into the entrance hall. "Karen and Gary, these are Stephen's children, Jill and Andy. Kids, meet Karen, Stephen's assistant, and Gary, our computer expert."

"Hey, Gary," Andy said, pushing past Jill. "Old Professor Greenly loaned me his computer while he's gone to New York. Can you help me run his tidal program? I can't get it to work."

"He left it to me as well," Jill countered.

"Hey, kids," Stephen called as he rounded the door into the entrance hall. "Let Gary at least take a breath before you hammer him with questions about the computer. Hi everybody. So nice to see you. Did you have any trouble finding the house?"

"Not at all. Stephen, who lives next door?" Janet queried.

"Oh," Stephen replied, laughing, "that's part of our house, too. Why don't I have Andy and Jill show you all around, while I do a few last chores in the kitchen. Better yet, Jill can show Janet and

Gary while Andy takes Karen. That way both of the kids will have a chance to be guides. I'll meet you when you're done."

Jill quickly ushered Gary and Janet toward the stairs to the left. "Come on," Andy said, motioning for Karen to follow him. "Let's start with the downstairs, that way we won't run into Jill."

"What's that?" asked Karen, pointing to what looked like a large brass whistle, mounted on a pipe next to the stairs.

"Here, push this button on the Band-Aid box, and pull the lever."

Karen looked at the old Johnson and Johnson box hooked to one of the logs, found the button and pushed it in. Nothing happened.

"Try it again," Andy urged, "but pull the lever on the whistle at the same time."

Karen tried again, and this time a loud blast filled the air. "Boy, that's loud," Karen said, letting the handle go.

"It's an old steam train whistle. Dad uses it to call us to dinner when we don't come the first time he calls. He usually only has to blow it once and we come running."

"I shouldn't wonder," Karen remarked, looking through the hall door. "Is this the dining room?"

"Yep. Those big display cases on each side of the table came from an old drug store in a town up north. They used to hold medicine and soap, and stuff like that."

Karen noticed the nicely set table and the display case on the right which was full of china. "What lovely dishes you have. I'm surprised your dad has so many," she remarked as she ran her hand along the glass fronts of the doors. "Do you use them often?"

"Not very, only when we have company, which isn't too often. Mostly me and Jill just have our friends over and we use the regular old dishes that we keep in the kitchen. You're the first lady

Dad's had here for dinner. Do you like my dad?"

"I like working for your dad, but I really haven't known him all that long."

"Well, he sure talks about you a lot. I think he likes you."

"What's down this hall?" Karen pointed, trying to change the subject.

"It's the front room."

"What a beautiful stone fireplace. Did your dad build this, too?"

"Dad built this whole house. Do you like the badger over the fireplace? His name is Buddy. We got him in Reedpoint, Montana, on the way back from one of Dad's field trips. At Christmas we put reindeer antlers on him and a Santa hat." Leaving the front room Andy quickly showed Karen the bathroom and guest room. Andy was eager to get on to the rec room. "You'll like the rec room," he beamed.

Andy led Karen through the kitchen where Stephen was bending over the sink. "Hi, Dad," Andy called out as he pulled Karen into the next room. "What do you think of the rec room?"

Karen stood at the edge of a large log room. The ceiling was peaked, not like the lower ceilings on the rest of the first floor. Massive log beams ran overhead and log rafters held up the wood plank roof. An old kitchen wood stove occupied the far corner of the room and next to that sat a player piano. The wood front had been removed from the piano and replaced with a glass front that someone had etched a delicate design into.

"Are these flowers?" Karen asked, looking at the design.

"They're morning glories. See, they gradually turn into butterflies. Look! Some leaves have flown away."

Karen bent down and looked closely at the etched design. As the vine grew longer, some of the leaves began to grow tiny antenna. Towards the end of the vine, some leaves were transformed into delicate butterflies. "It's beautiful, Andy, did—"

"Yeah, Dad did that too."

Turning around to look at the rest of the room, Karen noticed the long bar along one side. A long row of display cabinets filled the wall behind the bar. Upon walking closer, Karen noticed the cabinets were filled with all sorts of things. There were beehives, shells, rocks, old toys, souvenirs from trips, along with soda fountain glasses and banana split dishes. Looking down, Karen saw a full-sized soda fountain, complete with three soda water dispensers.

"How'd your dad get the soda fountain?"

"From the university, I guess, before I was born. Nobody wanted it since the cafeteria was switching to self-serve ice cream. Dad says Jill and I can make sodas for everyone after dinner. I hope you like sodas."

"I love them! Can I see the rest of the house?"

"The garage and workshop are boring, but wait until you see the dance hall."

"The dance hall?"

"Sure, come on!"

Andy led Karen through a storage room, out a door, across a short, covered walkway, into another door, and up a flight of stairs. The stairs led up to an enormous room. At one end was a piano, at the other end was a free standing cast-iron stove. The walls of the room were decorated with old farm tools, fencing swords, and cases filled with antiques. The ceiling was similar to the one in the rec room, only higher. The floor was made up of old boards, and the room reminded Karen of the loft of an old barn.

"Do you have dances here?" Karen asked, slightly overwhelmed by the size of the room.

"Jill and I have parties for our friends here, and sometimes Dad will dance with Jill, but Dad never has any grownups here. A friend of my dad's told me that Dad loved to dance—when he was younger—when he was married to my mother."

"Did you know your mother, Andy?"

"No, she went away when I was a baby. Dad won't talk about her, so don't ask him any questions. When I try to ask him anything about her, he changes the subject on me. I once asked Jill about her, but she only gets tears in her eyes and turns away. So, I don't bother to ask anymore. Hey, it's OK. Dad takes good care of us. I don't need a mother for anything. Let's go across the deck, we still have the attic playroom and my bedroom to see."

On the way to the attic playroom, Andy took a shortcut through Stephen's bedroom. Karen noticed pictures of Andy and Jill on the dresser, but no pictures of anyone that might have been his wife. Karen glanced into a side door. Inside was a large tub, surrounded by mirrors.

"Does your dad ever use that tub?"

"No, but he lets Jill and me use it."

Andy showed Karen the other bedrooms and bathroom on the second floor and then led the way to the attic. The attic was divided into sections including a dress-up area, pet shop, school, and house. At the other end of the play room there was a large train layout, complete with a tunnel, bridges, houses, road signs, and other paraphernalia. Shelves lined the walls and on them were bins with labels: Lincoln Logs, trucks, airplanes, doll house furniture, balls. Everything had a place and everything was in its place.

"I bet this is a popular place!" Karen exclaimed. "It makes me want to be a kid again."

"Uh-huh," Andy said. "The only problem is the clean up after we're done playing. Let's go down stairs now, OK?"

When they arrived back in the kitchen Stephen looked up.

"Did you give Karen a good tour, Andy?"

Before Andy had a chance to answer Karen exclaimed, "It's overwhelming, Stephen. Did you really do everything yourself?"

"Oh, once in a while I had some help, but it was mostly a family project. Here are the others. Let's visit until dinner is ready."

Gary excused himself and went off to help Andy with Professor Greenly's computer while Janet, Karen, Stephen, and Jill retired to the front room. They spent a pleasant afternoon together talking of the University, the kids' schools, and the boys Jill liked. Wonderful smells from the kitchen began to fill the house.

"What smells so good?" Karen asked, looking toward the kitchen. "It smells a little like yeast, but with a spicy scent to it. When is dinner?"

"Not for a while yet. It's a poor person's Northern Italian dish. Italian sausages simmered in wine, and served over polenta. All you're smelling now is the wine and sausages. The polenta gets cooked at the end, right before serving. The trick is to simmer it a long time so the smell saturates the logs. Then, we can enjoy the smell long into the evening."

"Polenta? I've heard of that before. Is it some type of pasta?" Janet wondered, now starting to notice the smell as well.

"It's not pasta, Janet," Jill replied. "It's just a fancy name for corn-meal mush."

"Well, plain or not, you sure can put it away when I make it," Stephen laughed. "Should I use the spoon?"

"The spoon?" asked Karen.

"The spoon," replied Stephen. "The spoon is never used for anything else. My aunt was one of those large, Italian women who had arms like a wrestler from rolling out pasta."

"And making polenta," Jill broke in. "she always stirred the polenta with the same spoon, so everyone in the family called it 'the polenta spoon.' The polenta is stirred as it boils, until the spoon will stand straight up in the pot without being held. Then it's done. Dad always uses the same large spoon."

After a couple of hours, Stephen left to complete the dinner by making the polenta. A short time later he blew three short blasts on the train whistle and called, "Dinner's on the table, come and get it while it's hot!"

CHAPTER THIRTEEN

ORPHAN GIRL

As the guests moved from the front room to the dining room, Gary and Andy came in from the computer room located just off of the kitchen. "Boy, does that smell good," Gary remarked, pulling up a chair and settling down at the table. "I've been smelling the food for hours, and am I ready to eat."

"Did you and Andy have any luck with Greenly's program?" Stephen asked.

"We sure did!" Andy said. "Gary can do anything on the computer. He sure is good! We got it running, and it even shows a graphic of the tidal bay and river. What's more, I can put restrictions anyplace I want and watch the changes in the currents. It's neat. The first thing I did was dam up the whole thing. It flooded everything!"

"Well, I'm not sure that's what the old professor had in mind when the program was written," Stephen said, putting a large bowl of steaming polenta on the table. "It was intended for serious research."

"What kind of research was he doing before he left?" Gary asked, reaching for the sausages.

"He was studying the tidal currents along the river, and how the salt water and fresh water mixed during the tidal surges. He said something about the currents changing, something about not understanding it."

"Remember where we dug for arrowheads, Dad?" Andy asked. "Remember how he said the currents had changed and now the better places to dig were uncovered at low tide? Don't you remember the nice arrowheads we found?"

"Yes, I do, now that you mention it. It's a shame, too. Now that he's put the project aside, I guess no one will ever know why the changes happened. Well, I don't suppose it's important, except to satisfy an old man's curiosity."

The conversation soon turned away from tidal currents and on to other subjects. Karen enjoyed the dinner and the relaxed conversation. She liked watching the interaction between Stephen and his children. Janet was right. They adored him, and he them. All three kidded each other about all sorts of things, but it was all good-natured and based on mutual respect. Karen noticed that both children listened carefully when Stephen spoke, but weren't afraid to voice differing views. Karen was wondering what the children would think if they knew about their dad's dream life when Stephen broke into her thoughts.

"Karen. You're so quiet. Judging by your appetite, though, I guess you like the food OK."

Such a remark about her eating coming from someone else would have offended her. Karen knew, however, that Stephen liked how she looked, at least in their dreams. So, she smiled and turned to answer him. "Oh, I'm just enjoying listening to everyone talk. Sometimes it's nice to just sit back. You're right about me liking the dinner. It's very good."

"I'm glad you like it, but save room for dessert. We're having sodas from the fountain, courtesy of Jill and Andy."

As the conversation moved away from her, Karen looked over the collection of plates, vases, and glasses in the display case opposite her. She supposed many had come from his wife, since it didn't seem as if a man would collect so many on his own. She wanted to ask about some of them, but was afraid Stephen would think she was prying about his marriage.

Her eyes slowly looked along the shelves, but stopped at an unusual vase on the top shelf. The vase was a light shade of purple, but the coloring was odd, almost transparent, and not evenly applied within the depth of the glass. The shape of the vase was almost as odd as the coloring. It looked as if it was formed from two pieces, like cheap bottles were. She wondered why someone would keep such a cheap vase. She stared at the vase for several minutes, trying to decide if she should ask Stephen.

"You look puzzled, Karen," Stephen said, after noticing the look on her face. "What are you thinking about?"

"Well," replied Karen, trying to quickly come up with something to say. "I'm curious about something in the display case. Do you mind me asking about it? I won't if you don't want me to."

"No, it's all right," Stephen said, as the muscles tightened noticeably in his jaw. "What would you like to know about?"

"The odd colored vase in the top, right corner. Is it an antique?"

Stephen visibly relaxed as soon as he heard the question. "Yes, yes it is an antique."

"Tell them about your uncle from Montana, Dad," Jill piped in. "It's an interesting story."

"Yeah, Dad, I'd like to hear about him, too," added Andy.

"Well, if everyone doesn't mind listening to a story, I'll try not to make it too long. My Uncle Joe was born before the turn of the century on a large farm in southern Montana, not far from Yellowstone Park. Farming was hard work then, not much in the way of machinery was available to ease the daily burdens. Anyway, he didn't much like the work. One of his chores was to keep the sickles sharpened that were used to cut the wheat. Daydreaming away, he wasn't paying attention and lopped off the end of his finger. He was afraid to tell his father, so he took off for town.

"He ended up sleeping in the hayloft over a livery stable. At that time only a few automobiles were on the road, and if anything happened to one of them it was hauled to the livery stable, like a sick horse. It wasn't too long after he arrived at the livery stable that a team of horses towed in a broken car. Well, the livery owner and the blacksmith couldn't figure out how to fix it, but my uncle figured it out and had the car back running in a few hours. The owner of the stable was so impressed with my uncle that he offered him room and board if he would stay and help as a mechanic."

"How old was your uncle when he left home?" Karen asked.

"I think he was not more than twelve at the time."

"Only twelve? Didn't his parents go looking for him?" Karen returned, somewhat astonished that he was so young.

"He had lots of brothers and sisters, and I've heard that his parents knew where he had gone and probably weren't concerned as long as he was taken care of. Besides, I think they were tired of his complaining and maybe hoped he had found something he liked better. It turned out he was a natural born genius at fixing anything mechanical. He could have stayed working at the livery stable, but he got caught up in the gold fever that was sweeping Montana. Everyone either knew someone who had struck it rich, or had tried to find gold themselves. My uncle took off with an old prospector who showed up at the stable one day to get his Model T fixed. This prospector had made his fortune in Alaska before the turn of the century, and now was spending his retirement criss-crossing the west looking for the famous lost mines."

"Ones like Death Valley Scotty's?" Andy asked, filling his mouth with a large spoonful of polenta and red gravy.

"Ones like that, but my uncle told me there were rumors about lots of lost mines that now are long forgotten. Anyway, Uncle Joe ended up going with the prospector out into the western deserts for most of a year. It was during that time that he found that vase. Actually, it's not a vase, but a large olive jar. The odd color comes from being in the sun. Some cheaper grades of glass react to the sun that way, turning that odd shade of purple. Jill, why don't you get it down and let Karen look at it. Hey! If everyone's done, let's go for sodas."

Karen stayed behind the others as they moved into the rec room. She held the jar lightly in her hands, slowly turning it over to see all the different shades of purple. Am I like this jar? She thought to herself, I was plain and ordinary like this jar was, but the sun has turned me into something of beauty and value, like it did to this vase. Reluctantly putting down the vase, Karen hurried to catch up with the others.

While Jill and Andy were making sodas on request, Karen was still thinking about the purple vase and Stephen's uncle. "What did your uncle do after looking for the lost mines, Stephen?" Karen asked after giving Jill her order for a soda. "Did he make his fortune in gold?"

"Well, he did, but not by mining," Stephen replied, probing his soda for the cherry that had sunk to the bottom of the glass. "He became a mining engineer. He worked for a famous mine in Butte, Montana. Now that mine is a part of an exhibit that includes several of the inventions my uncle developed for mining. I haven't been there, but I've heard that there's a ghost town made up of old buildings that were trucked into the site. I think there might be a mining car ride, or something like that, too."

"Is the mine still open?"

"No, all the gold mines closed down when the easy to mine gold was gone. Actually, copper became the important mineral, not gold. Now, not even copper is important, since all the easy to mine copper is gone as well."

"Hey, Dad," Andy interjected, while carefully adding several cherries to the top of his soda. "What's the name of the mine that Uncle Joe worked at, the one at the museum you're talking about?"

"It's the Orphan Girl Mine. It was named that because of the accidents in the mine that killed so many miners."

Karen's eyes locked onto Gary's. Gary silently mouthed "Butte, Orphan Girl!!!," then put his finger to his lips.

"What was that name again?" Karen asked, trying to keep the quiver out of her voice.

"Orphan Girl. Why don't we sit down and enjoy our sodas."

Karen could hardly pay attention to the conversation. Her mind was racing with everything that had happened. Orphan Girl, she thought. Was it a coincidence, or something more? Karen kept looking over at Gary, but he was acting perfectly normal, talking and seemingly enjoying himself. Karen wondered if she was jumping to conclusions.

After an hour, Janet got up, stretched, and said, "Well, it's been a lovely afternoon but I have to run some errands in the morning. Gary, would it be all right if we headed for home now?"

"Actually there is something I want to show Andy on the computer before I leave. I'm not sure when I'll get back out here, so I'd like to do it now. Why don't you take my car home. I'll ride back with Karen, if that's OK with her?"

"Sure," Karen replied, sensing the hint in Gary's voice. "Gary can help Andy on the computer, and I'll help with the dishes. Why don't you take Gary's car?"

It didn't take long to talk Janet into borrowing Gary's car for the night. After thanking Stephen, Jill, and Andy for dinner, she passed through the gate and out into the night.

"Come on, Gary," Andy said. "Let's work on the computer!"

Andy grabbed Gary's hand to pull him into the computer room, but Gary turned instead to Stephen. "Stephen, Karen and I have something to tell you, but I'm afraid that you'll think we're nuts."

"What?" answered Stephen.

"We have something to tell you," broke in Karen, "but we're afraid of what you'll think about it."

"Well, the best thing," Stephen said, worrying that something was seriously wrong, or worse yet, that they were in love, "is to just tell me what's on your minds. Let's move into the front room, where we can sit down and be comfortable."

Gary, Stephen, and Karen quickly moved into the front room and sat down. Andy and Jill followed close behind. Both caught the sharp glance from Stephen, but kept coming right into the room anyway. Despite the look from their dad, they knew from the tone of the voices that something good was going to be said, and they didn't want to miss it. Stephen, sensing their determination, relented, but not before admonishing them. "OK, you can stay, but nothing we say here leaves here—do you understand?"

"OK," both Jill and Andy nodded, thrilled to be included in whatever might be coming next.

"So," Stephen said, turning his attention to Gary and Karen, who seemed to shrink in their chairs under his gaze, "what's this all about?"

"It's going to sound crazy," Karen started, "but when we heard the words 'Orphan Girl' and 'Butte' everything fell into place!"

"What fell into place?"

"Fulton. We think he may have been killed because of what he knew!"

"Killed!" replied Stephen, caught off guard. "What did he know that he would've been killed for?"

"We don't know what he knew," Karen admitted.

"Then how do you know that what he knew might have killed him?"

"Let me try explaining it," Gary interjected, leaning forward in his seat. "After Fulton left, I found that he had hidden files containing garbled station reports. He had saved them out for a reason. We found a message he sent to the National Weather Service asking about them, but he didn't receive a reply, at least as far as we can tell. What made Karen and me suspicious was the fact that he went to all the trouble to hide the files. Why not keep them in the open if he—"

"Karen's told all this to me before," Stephen interrupted, relieved that this was all they wanted to tell him about. "You guys are jumping to conclusions."

"I don't think so," Karen interrupted. "Gary's been decoding the messages and they're in some type of secret code."

"Secret code?" Stephen asked.

"Yes, we're sure that the scrambled station messages are in some type of code. Someone is sending messages all over the world using the worldwide circuits that distribute weather information. Anyone can receive them with the right equipment. Who would ever find out?" Karen continued.

"Who's this someone that's sending the messages?"

"We don't know," Karen answered.

"What?"

"We don't know," Karen repeated. "Remember the puzzle? The one that the hacker who broke into our computers left in everyone's home directory? The solution spelled out Jim Fulton! Gary's sure the hacker was looking for evidence that we're trying to break the code."

"Is that true, Gary?" Stephen asked.

"It's true about the puzzle but I don't really know what the motive was for the breaking into our system. The person who broke in went to all the trouble to copy my trace back files. He, or she, wouldn't do that unless they wanted to find out everything I've been doing on the computer. But, they didn't find out I'd been trying to break the code, because I'd moved the code breaking program to the new, faster computer that wasn't yet connected to the network."

"Gary's sure that they left a program on our system to report back on our activities," Karen added.

"And," Gary continued, not giving Stephen a chance to reply, "whoever broke in couldn't help but brag, so he left Jim Fulton's name as a calling card."

"Did you find the program they left on the computer?"

"I don't want to try for fear they will find out that we suspect them."

"Them?"

"Yes, them," Karen broke in. "The killers. We have to be careful! Gary and I thought we were jumping to conclusions, too, but not anymore! Gary managed to decode a station name, and it's Butte, Montana. He decoded two other words also. They were Orphan Girl. We thought it was all nonsense because the words didn't mean anything, but not now! It fits, Orphan Girl—Butte—."

"Gary, did you actually break those words from the code?" Stephen interjected.

"Well, yes and no," Gary answered, not sure of what exactly to say. "The code breaking program gave some possibilities. We know the station name begins with a B, but it could be lots of names besides Butte, Montana. The name Orphan Girl came up, but the program listed several other possibilities. Now I'm not so sure."

"I'm sure!" Andy excitedly added, no longer able to keep quiet. "It's an international crime ring. They killed Fulton because they were afraid he would bring attention to their method of sending messages. They felt they had to check on Gary to see if he was still suspicious of the scrambled messages, but left the puzzle to make it look like some hacker did it. The guy's some type of psycho. He left Jim Fulton's name just to toy with Gary. Gary broke the code and now they're going to kill Gary in some horrible, grues --"

"Andy!" Stephen cut him short before he could finish the word 'gruesome.' "Slow down. Everyone slow down and take a breath. Let me think! Someone, we don't know who, possibly, and I'm emphasizing possibly, killed Fulton. We don't have any proof that he is even dead. These people are evil, if they even exist. We don't even know that they do exist. Someone broke into the computer system, but we can't be sure because, if we actually are sure, then the people that we don't know really exist might kill Gary. All this is tied to a mine in Butte, Montana that has been closed for over sixty years. The decoded messages could fit hundreds of other places too. Orphan Girl could mean anything. Can we be sure about anything? Yes. Jim Fulton did disappear. He was curious about the scrambled station reports. He sent an inquiry to the Weather Service. Someone broke into our computer system. Butte and Orphan Girl might or might not be part of a coded message. But, all this hardly adds up to murder."

Gary and Karen settled back in their seats, feeling a little embarrassed for making so much out of the few solid facts they had. Jill, quiet while all this was going on, stood up. "Sure it's farfetched, but not totally impossible. Dad, did Uncle Joe leave anything that might tell us something about the Orphan Girl mine?"

"Not much. All he left me was the purple olive jar, his pan and pick, and a few samples of ore from the mine."

"Where are the ore samples?" Jill prodded.

"I have them," Andy replied, hurrying off to hunt through his room for them.

Karen, Jill, Gary, and Stephen could hear sounds of the room above their heads being ripped apart as drawers flew open and articles of various weights hit the floor. A muffled, "I found them!" was followed by the sound of flying feet on the stairs. "Here they are," he exclaimed, as he flew into the room and handed them to Stephen.

Stephen opened the box and looked in. Several pieces of what looked like rocks were lying loose in the bottom. One rock was wrapped in an old paper. Stephen handed around the loose rocks, but no one could see anything interesting about them. The rock wrapped in the paper was heavier than the others, but really didn't look much different.

"Read what's on the paper, Dad," Jill said.

Unfolding the paper, Stephen read, "Missouri Hydrologic Bulletin. Daily Precipitation Station Changes. Wise River, Montana, moved one quarter mile NE of former location on August 18, 1927. No changes in Lat. or Long. or station name."

"Is that all?" Andy asked, slumping dejectedly back into his chair. "I was hoping it would be a clue, or something."

"Hey," Stephen said, feeling sorry for Andy, "I've got a great idea. I've wanted to take you kids to Butte for a long time to show you where Uncle Joe lived and worked. Other things kept coming up, and I kept putting it off. I don't think there is anything to this crime business, but so what? We can poke around and have some fun. I've got time after summer quarter finishes in three weeks. Andy, we can hunt for rocks and arrowheads, and Jill, we can take in some western art. Well, what do you think?"

"Sure, Dad, we'd love to go," chorused both kids.

"Gary, you can come if you want, and Karen, we'd love to have you come, too."

"Thanks for the invitation," Gary replied, "but I've got lots of programming to do before autumn quarter."

"What about you, Karen?" Stephen asked again.

Before she could answer, Jill broke in. "Please come, Karen. It'd be nice for me to have another woman along to balance out all the men. Won't you come?"

"Well, if my boss will give me the time off, I'll come."

"Then it's settled," Stephen proclaimed. "We're going!"

The ringing of the phone interrupted the excited chatter. As he picked up the receiver, Stephen's face turned grim. "You're kidding?" was all he said, besides. "I'll tell them," before he hung up.

"It's bad news. Gary, you and Karen will have to go and pick up Janet at the Crossroads Store. She stopped for some aspirin, and when she left Gary's car to go in the store, someone stole it."

CHAPTER FOURTEEN

SATISFACTION

E SLOWLY SAT BACK in his chair. He looked for a long time at his long, slender fingers, holding them motionless against the dark background of his room. *Some are born for hard work, some are born for a life of ease, some are born to create beauty, some, like me, are born to help them create that beauty.*

He lowered his hands to his lap and remained in that position for several long minutes. *At least feeding time had finally come again,* he thought. *Now I won't have to feel so bad when only I can be fed.* Glancing once more at his hands, he spoke out loud. "Some are born to help others create beauty."

Later, when he was flying over the French countryside, he thought how beautiful the graveyards looked in the moonlight. He flew lower to look at a large tomb that was mostly underground, but had small windows covered with grating protruding above the surface.

Lovely, he thought, looking inside. *Human bones are so beautiful. I wonder how they died? I think I'll come back when I have more time—maybe they will tell me. Yes, I think they will.*

CHAPTER FIFTEEN

SERGEANT GRANT

JANET, GARY, STEPHEN, AND KAREN watched Sergeant Grant sift through the stack of papers. Stephen thought Grant was too young to be a sergeant in the police force, but then lately, every professional he had contact with seemed younger than himself. Gary wondered if Sergeant Grant would be able to get his car back. Janet hoped this meeting would be over quickly so she could hurry back to her regular routine. Karen eyed the gun in the holster hanging from her belt. Could I use that to kill someone, if I had to? Could this Sergeant? Has this Sergeant?

Finding what she was looking for, Sergeant Emily Grant looked up at the group gathered before her. The people she dealt with always seemed to look the same at these meetings. Bankers, scientists, doctors, mechanics, teachers, unknowns, and well-knowns. They all had that same anxious, nervous, but hopeful look. She hated to watch those looks turn to disappointment, but lately her job as liaison to victims was mostly to disappoint them. She glanced back at Stephen. His eyes caught her attention. They weren't anxious or nervous, but looked at her with intense interest. She didn't want to stare at his eyes, but she could hardly keep from looking.

She forced herself to pull away and look back at the others.

"I've called you together for this meeting this morning to explain what we know about the theft of Gary's automobile," Grant began. "You might wonder why more of you are here besides the owner of the automobile. I've found that it's better to have everyone, even those remotely involved in the crime, come to these meetings. That way, there is less misunderstanding later, and the victim has additional people to talk to and support him. Most of you might not realize it, but there is a subculture within our city and surrounding areas whose values don't reflect yours. You might find it hard to believe, but in this city if you want someone killed, there are people who will do it. You might sit around at lunch talking about sports or the latest movies. Some people in this city sit around at lunch casually talking about robbery and murder for hire, and they don't even get indigestion. It's so much a part of their lives and their values are so different, that I find that it is hard for most people outside of that culture to understand it. Anyway, the police department is lucky that some members of that culture don't mind working as paid informants for the city. I know that some citizens don't like the idea of paying people they consider lowlifes for information, but it is the only way the police department can keep up with crime. It's not pretty, but it works.

"So, this brings us to your case. The pattern of the theft of your automobile, Gary, fits the method used by a man who is presently going by the name of Samuel Jones. He works by himself. He works at night, when, if he's seen, it's difficult for a witness to get a good description. He haunts fast food and convenience stores looking for late model cars that can be quickly sold to 'strippers' who divide up the car so it can't be traced. We know who he is, but we can't get enough evidence to arrest him. Oh, we could arrest him, but what's the use? We couldn't make it stick. In cases like this, we hope that the suspect will eventually slip up, but in the meantime we pressure him as much as possible."

"How do you do that?" Stephen asked. "What kind of leverage can you have over someone like that?"

"Not a lot," Grant replied. "But we can put the word out that we know what he's doing, and that we're paying informants. Sometimes that is enough to send a criminal out of our area, or make him slip up. In this case, Jones had so far proven immune to this pressure."

"Why 'had'?" Stephen interjected.

"Our informants tell us he's vanished. That's somewhat puzzling to us because he didn't seem to want to budge, or seem likely to slip up. But these types are hard to understand. Maybe he's found a new girlfriend in another town, or has gotten tired of his present one and left the area to get away from her. However, we're told his girlfriend was caught off guard as much as we were when he left."

"What about my car?" Gary asked worriedly. "Was any trace of it found?"

"No," Grant replied, shifting some of the papers to the top of the pile. "The parts from your make and model of car are in high demand. Jones knew what he was doing. People who strip a car like yours will take off all the salable parts that can't be traced, then crush all the rest and sell it for scrap. I'm sorry. From our experience, I don't think that you will ever see your car again. With Jones gone, I don't see how we have any chance of solving this case. We've put the word out to surrounding cities. He might turn up, but who knows when or where. He might even give up stealing for a living, which is unlikely, but it could happen. The best thing is to get on with your life. I can't answer for your insurance company, but in cases like this, they typically wait a few days to see if the car was simply taken by amateurs for a joy ride or for the radio.

If it doesn't turn up, they'll settle."

"Oh—you asked earlier about Jim Fulton," Grant said, putting away the papers into a folder, and standing up. "Nothing new. We're considering that investigation closed. He's taken off, and if a person doesn't want to be found, that's about the end of it. We have too many other, more serious cases to work on. If someone cared enough, his family for instance, they could hire a private detective who most likely could find him, but they're expensive. Actually it's cheaper to wait until he decides to turn up."

"Could there be any connection between the disappearance of Jones and Fulton?" Karen asked.

Grant, caught by surprise at the question, took a few minutes to think. "I don't see how there could be. We look for similarities between cases to connect them. Jim Fulton didn't have anything we know of in common with Jones. Neither did his disappearance. Besides, we have no reason to believe that the fact that both are gone had anything to do with criminal acts against them. Do you have any reason to think otherwise?" Grant ended, looking more closely at Karen.

"Not really," Karen quickly answered, feeling somewhat embarrassed by her question. "I just asked before I thought it through."

CHAPTER SIXTEEN

CLOSE ENCOUNTERS
OF THE ULTIMATE KIND

KAREN LAY BACK in the sand, her feet slowly digging into the warm, top layer and down into the cooler, damper layer below. Then she slid her toes back into the warmth again. She shuddered as the warm sand flowed over her cold feet. She tipped her head back, digging her feet once again into the coolness of the lower sand. She looked at the small, white clouds floating by overhead. With their darker undersides and crisp white tops outlined against the blue sky, Karen thought they looked like cut out clouds on a child's paste-up picture.

"Is this all real, Stephen?" Karen asked. "The white of the clouds is so brilliant, the blue of the sky is so vivid! The bottoms of the clouds are perfectly flat! It's all too perfect to be real. You must have made it all up just for me."

Stephen looked at Karen. He enjoyed how she lay naked, but unashamed before him. He liked to watch her breasts as she moved her feet through the sand in a rhythmic motion. Each movement of her legs and feet changed the shape of her breasts in subtle ways.

Small ways—ways that made Stephen long to touch them softly, so softly that he wouldn't change their slow movement, but just enough to feel the movement with his fingers. When she rose slightly and lifted her arm to point at the clouds, Stephen watched her nipples cascade downward, then move outward in a smooth curving motion as her breasts suddenly filled out in a new shape.

"They are too perfect to be real!" Stephen replied to her query, looking intently at her.

"Not my breasts," Karen laughed. "The clouds. I wanted to know if you made them up, or if they are real."

"The clouds—oh—you mean the cumulus humulis drifting by overhead," Stephen said, quickly glancing up at the clouds, but returning to look at Karen. "They're fair-weather cumulus. I thought they would add a nice touch to the blue sky. Oh, they're real all right. I've tried to improve on natural clouds, but I can't beat the real thing. Would you like a different kind of cloud?"

"No, these clouds are fine for now," Karen replied, laying back down on the sand, continuing the motions with her feet and legs. Karen enjoyed having Stephen look at her. "What do you find so interesting about me today, Stephen, that you find me more fun to watch than the clouds?"

Stephen looked directly into Karen's eyes. He spoke with a clear, firm voice, devoid of any shame or embarrassment. "It's your breasts, Karen. It's the way they move to the rhythm of your feet and legs. It's the slight changes in the curves that define them. It's how the curves take up the light, and how the light changes when they move, and how that movement of light changes their shape, and their shape changes in time to the beating of my heart. When you raised up and your breasts suddenly cascaded downward, like two identical avalanches, your nipples like twin skiers riding the crest of the white snow as they curved downward and outward—

I felt faint, they were so beautiful. And your calves. The curves of the back of your calves also change with the rhythm of your feet. The soft hairs on your thighs suddenly appear as the part of your legs in the shade rotates into the sun, then they disappear into the darkness with the rhythm of your feet. Watching you, I've memorized every hair on your thighs, every curve of your calves, each small movement of your breasts." Stephen pulled his gaze away from Karen and looked out over the blue-green ocean, watching colorful fish swimming along the sunlit, translucent tops of the breaking waves.

"See those fish, Karen? See how they move through the translucent part of the breaking waves? The sun and the fish are like you. The fish swim because they have to. They could no more stop swimming then the sun could stop rising. The sun shines and illuminates the tops of the waves. And neither realizes together what beauty they combine to make. So Karen, your feet only strive to feel the coolness and warmth of the sand, but that striving compels the curves of your calves to change, and the movement of your calves compels your thighs to flex, bringing each hair into the sun, and the flexing of your thighs causes your breasts to move and change shape. None have the purpose of beauty in their will, but still, it's beauty they create." Stephen fell silent, lost in his thoughts.

A sudden breeze blew fine particles of sand across the beach in small whirls, creating little ridges in the sand, and then just as quickly erasing them. The breeze was warm as it swirled around Karen, dusting sand slowly upon her. Karen could feel each individual grain touch her skin like tiny, warm fingers which were afraid to do more than quickly touch, then pull away. The touches of the sand became stronger as Karen ceased the movement of her feet and lay still, her head resting in a cradle in the sand, her body aware of every touch.

"The wind wants me, Stephen!" Karen gasped. "Will it take me here?"

"Not today," Stephen replied, standing up and brushing the sand from his legs and back. "Not today. Someone waits for you, and that someone will be jealous if the wind takes you first. Come. We need to start if we will reach there in time, and we have a lot to do before we reach there."

Stephen reached down, extended his hand toward hers, and gently pulled Karen to her feet. The fine sand that had clung to her body now fell away in disappointment as the breeze stopped its swirling and returned to blowing along the beach.

"Who's waiting for me, Stephen? Is it you? Are you the one who'll be waiting for me?" Karen asked, trying to hide the anticipation in her voice.

"No, Karen," Stephen said in a low voice, turning away, as he led her along the beach. "I can't."

Karen wanted to ask why, but was so struck by the sorrow and hurt in his reply that the words died in her throat and she fell silent beside him.

"Oh, Karen," Stephen said, as he finally found his own voice. "The person who waits for you loves you, too."

"Do you love me, Stephen?" Karen whispered.

"I couldn't share this dream with anyone I didn't love," Stephen whispered back, as he turned Karen to face him. "But, Karen, I can't love you like a man needs to love a women — should love a woman."

As Karen looked up at Stephen, tears fell from the corners of her eyes, picking up small pieces of sand that still clung to her cheeks. Stephen reached out to brush them aside. As he moved his fingers across her cheeks, they came to softly rest on her lips. Karen gently kissed his fingers as he drew them away.

"Don't cry, Karen. I want you to be with this person. It would be selfish to keep you for myself. I love you so much, so unselfishly, that I'm willing to give you to another, and that person wants you so badly. In some ancient cultures, when a woman loved a man, or a man loved a woman, and they couldn't be with them, they would pay to send them to someone they could be with. It was an expression of their love, but only of the purest kind of unselfish love. That's the love I have for you."

"I love you too, Stephen," Karen replied as he led her away from the beach. "But not in the way you love me. I love you like a woman loves a man, but not unselfishly, like you say you love me. I guess that there are some things I can't understand."

"Karen, understand that we're together today, that this dream is as real as my love for you, that we're sharing each other, and that I promise I'll never do anything to hurt you, or cause you to feel sad. Today is for us, for me, but especially for you. Let's not analyze it, let's enjoy it!"

The path turned inland, away from the beach, climbed over small sand dunes covered with tufts of grass and low leafy plants. Gradually the sand dunes became fewer, and the path wound around dry hills of golden brown grass. After a while the sound of the waves on the beach was lost in the sound of the wind blowing through the dry grass. "Do you mind the color of the grass, Karen?" Stephen asked, lightly holding her hand as they walked side by side.

"It's pretty," Karen remarked in reply. "There are so many shades of gold and brown that I can hardly look away. The sky is so blue in contrast to the golds. Did you want it to be these colors?"

"This grass was once green and new, like you were when I first shared my dreams with you. As your experiences grew, so did these grasses. As you matured in your feelings, so did the grasses mature.

Now the grasses on these hills have ripened. See how the end of the stalks are full of the life of the new grass. These grasses are ready to burst, and by bursting they take on a new life. You're now ripe in experience like these grasses. It's time for you to experience the transformation that only the one who waits for you can give you. That one loves you more than I could ever love you."

"How does this person know me?"

"Do you play a musical instrument, Karen?"

"I played the piano when I was younger, but haven't kept it up."

"Did you ever play on other pianos, besides the one you practiced on?"

"Sometimes, but not too often. Why?"

"I play the piano. Each piano is different, and has its own sound. But more importantly, each piano responds to the touch of the keys in a different and unique way."

"How do you mean?" Karen asked, wondering why Stephen was telling her this.

"When I first play on a new piano, I start slowly, trying out all the octaves. I need to discover how the keys need to be played. Some pianos need to be played hard in the lower octaves, but oh—so gently and carefully in the higher notes. Others don't respond to hard touches at all, but need to be almost caressed. When I discover how a piano responds, then I can become more bold in my playing, confident that the piano will come alive under my touch. Each song needs to be played in a unique way, a way that is different for each piano. On one piano a piece might need a slow build up to a strong and sudden ending. The same piece, on a different piano, might need strength throughout, but can only come alive with a muted and delicate ending."

"Does this person who waits for me play the piano?"

Stephen continued, not directly answering her question.

"When a man makes love to a woman for the first time, it's like sitting down to play on a new piano. He has to go slowly, learning how she responds to his touch, to his voice. Each woman is different, and, like a musical instrument, responds in different ways. When a man finds that way, that combination of voice and movement, she becomes alive under his hands. A pianist can hardly ever sit down at a strange piano and play it right off without first searching for its strengths and weaknesses. Once, in a great while it happens. Today that will happen for you, Karen."

"What will happen for me?" Karen asked, suddenly becoming very sleepy.

"Have you seen the movie 'Close Encounters of the Third Kind'? There is a scene in it where the scientist's computer begins to communicate with the computer on the spaceship. Do you remember that scene from the movie?"

"Partly. Is it when the computer starts out by playing the simple sequence of notes sent by the spaceship?"

"Yes, but remember how rapidly the computers go from playing the simple tune to playing the extremely complicated and rapid sequences of notes? It's almost spontaneous. It happened because the computers could learn everything about each other in a split second. So will the person that waits for you, when you are taken. They will know everything about how to 'play' you. In honor of the movie, I call the experience that you will shortly have, 'Close Encounters of the Ultimate Kind,' for there are no encounters that can exceed this one in our lucid dreams."

"Stephen," Karen responded in a sleepy voice. "I'm tired from walking, and I'm not paying attention to what you're saying. Can we rest?"

"Yes," Stephen said, as they rounded the crest of another hill. He pointed to a small, earth-colored house. "I think we can rest there."

Inside, the house was full of the good smell of hot food. Karen noticed that a pot of vegetable soup simmered on the old kitchen stove.

"Strange," thought Karen. "it's my favorite kind."

The table was set, as if whoever lived there was expecting company for lunch. The door from the kitchen to a side room was open. Karen looked in and saw a bed, the covers turned back, as if waiting for someone. The bed was covered with a beautiful comforter, patterned with the delicate wildflowers from Karen's earlier lucid dreams.

"I'm so tired, Stephen. Could I lay here for a few minutes? Would you mind?"

"This bed was made for you, Karen. When you lucid dream, fly by the ocean, along the beach. Come down to the beach when you see a patch of sand that shimmers. Land on that sand and I'll meet you in the air," Stephen instructed, as he laid her gently on the bed.

"How can I lucid dream inside this dream, and the sand's not in the air --?" she asked as her sleepy voice trailed off ---.

137

CHAPTER SEVENTEEN

KAREN

KAREN LOOKED DOWN at the beach. She could see the indentations in the sand where she and Stephen had lain. Karen remembered how cool the lower layers of the sand had felt. She remembered the sudden surge of feeling that spread from her feet, up her legs, and into her torso as she rhythmically moved her feet between the two layers of sand. She remembered the fish, outlined in the translucent upper part of the waves, and the soft touch of the windblown sand. She remembered Stephen. Had he said he loved her? He loved her, but couldn't love her. If he loved her so much, why couldn't he love her like a man loves a woman, like a woman needs to be loved by a man? She remembered the soft touch of Stephen's fingers on her lips. Tears fell from her eyes. Small beads of sadness, dropping toward the beach, glittering in the sunlight as they fell.

"Oh my tears, consecrate this beach where Stephen first said he loved me. Bless it for the future, our future ---"

Karen watched as her tears touched the beach. To her astonishment, where each tear landed ripples radiated outwards, like ripples from a stone thrown into a pond. But these weren't like water ripples, rather they were like little waves of shimmering sand. As her tears continued to fall, Karen saw the individual shimmering patches spread outward, then merge into a shimmering mass of sand waves.

"Go to the beach, into the shimmering sand--," a voice softly said.

Transfixed by the array of colors, Karen descended toward the beach. As she touched the surface, the colors whirled around her, and she continued to plunge through the beach, deeper and deeper into the sand. Suddenly, she burst through into darkness.

"Karen! I've been waiting for you," Stephen called out, as he caught her hand.

Finding herself unexpectedly in the air, Karen held tightly to his hand. He squeezed hers as they glided over the dark ground, far below. The sun was just rising, and the first rays were hitting the higher hills as the golden hills of ripened grass were coming alive with the touch of the sun. Suddenly the sun rose above the far hills, and the light warmed Karen's face.

"The morning light becomes you, Karen", Stephen said, deftly guiding her to the right. "You are truly beautiful! Sunlight is the only makeup that should ever touch your face—only the wind should brush your hair—. Come. We need to hurry. She will be waking up soon."

"Who?"

"The one who waits for you—look!"

Far below Karen, tucked between the hills, was a small, earth-colored house. The sun was just beginning to strike the windows. Smoke rose from the stovepipe. As Stephen guided her closer, doves that had been roosting under the eaves flew upward, their white underbellies catching the sun as they turned in unison, back toward the ocean. Stephen brought them to rest before the door.

"Knock, Karen."

Karen felt the touch of his hand lighten, then the touch was gone. "Stephen!" Karen called, but as she turned, all she saw were the doves in the distance. Karen faced the door and knocked. A pleasant, familiar voice called to her from inside.

"Karen, don't be afraid. I love you as much as you love yourself."

Karen began to tremble. She wanted to run, but the voice had seemed to freeze her where she stood. Suddenly she felt light-headed as the door opened into the room, and the rich smell of soup mixed with the scent of wild flowers filled her senses.

It's my scent! Karen thought, amazed. It's the scent of the flowers I lay in!

Strong feelings washed over her—of love, of acceptance, of desire. Her knees began to buckle, just as a hand reached out and drew her inside.

"Don't tremble—oh—no—you're afraid—don't be—oh—you are so beautiful—I want you so much—."

Karen looked up. Holding her hand was the most beautiful woman she had ever seen. She reached out to touch her face. The woman reached out an identical hand, and at the same time touched Karen in the same way. As Karen brought her fingers gently down her cheek, she felt the other fingers move the same way. Her fingers brushed the lips of the other woman, just as she felt soft fingers brush hers. She moved her fingers down her throat, down over the curves of her breast, and stopped. Fingers stopped on her breasts. She could feel and touch at the same time. Karen had never felt such emotion swell within her. This woman—this woman whom she loved, and needed— knew how to touch her like she had only known to touch herself. As she began again to feel the soft contours of her breasts, and felt hers being traced in the same way, in ways only she had known, Karen whispered,

"How do you know me so well?"

"Look at me Karen—," she murmured, while they continued tracing the outline of each other's breasts. "Look closely at me."

Karen looked, and the motion of her hands stopped. "You're me —but—how—how—?"

As Karen's hands began to fly faster over her body, she felt every touch on herself. Every touch she felt on herself was intensified by touching her. They drew each other close, their nipples brushing lightly together. When they kissed, each touch of their lips was perfect. Everywhere they placed their hands was exactly the per- fect place. Everywhere they placed their lips was ecstasy. Every place they explored was done as they wanted. All this they knew without speaking a word. Their touches ebbed and flowed, to the rhythm of a song, a song only they knew.

To touch and feel that touch—, Karen thought. "Stephen! Stephen!" she cried. "Stephen—thank you—."

As their feelings swelled, the room became dark around them. All their attention was on themselves. The strong sensual emo- tions, combined with love and complete acceptance, were so intense for them that they cried out several times in the same voice.

"Stop --stop -- too strong ---- oh -- oh -- don't continue -- no -- don't stop --."

Minutes spread into hours. They lost all sense of time. The only time that mattered was the present. Now, incredibly strong feelings were rushing toward them. They, in turn, rushed towards those feelings, rushed to embrace them.

Afterwards, they lay in each other's arms. The rich smell of their bodies covered them. They didn't speak, as each knew what the other was thinking. Their bodies were one. They fell asleep together.

KAREN

Where am I? Karen thought, as she slowly stretched her whole body and felt the soft warmth of the sheets wrapped around her. She opened her eyes, but only for an instant. She thought she saw her hands laying on a bed of delicate flowers, and she thought she smelled the rich smell of soup, mixed with her scent. Then she fell back into a deep sleep.

Karen awoke again, this time she was in her own bed. She felt so wonderful that she lay very still hoping not to lose how she felt. She lay so still that as the hours of the day passed, and the sun set outside her window, she fell back asleep without ever having moved.

144

CHAPTER EIGHTEEN

EASTWARD

"**D**AD?" JILL ASKED, throwing her suitcase into the trunk of their car. "Do you think there is anything to the suspicions that Karen and Andy have?"

"No, honey," Stephen replied, "but, I know how much fun it is for Andy to think about it. There's no harm in letting him dream. That's what sets us apart from the animals. Besides, I've always wanted to see where your great uncle lived. This is a good opportunity to do just that."

"Will Karen be coming soon?" Jill asked, looking out of their driveway and down towards the road.

"Do you like her, honey?" Stephen inquired, without answering her question.

"Do you, Dad?" Jill asked in return, without answering his.

"I do. Yes, I'm starting to like her quite a bit."

"I do too, Dad. I'm looking forward to having her on the trip with us."

"Gary's bringing her out anytime now," Stephen said, also glancing down the road. "He's got a loaner car from the insurance company. I suppose his car is gone for good. Sometimes life is so strange ---."

"They're coming," Andy exclaimed, interrupting Stephen's thoughts with a cry from the second story window. "I see them turning the corner across from the red barn."

Stephen and Jill looked up expectantly as Gary's loaner car drove through the gate and into the driveway. Andy was down the stairs and up to the parking car before Stephen and Jill.

"Gary! Karen! We're all packed! We're ready to go! Come on Karen! Montana, here we come!" Andy cried as he pulled Karen out of the car.

"Hold on," Gary admonished. "You can't go to Montana without Karen's clothes!"

"Sorry!" Andy yelled, the admonition not slowing his enthusiasm at all. "Let me take your luggage, Karen -- Montana -- boy, oh boy!"

Karen's bags were loaded along with the few items Jill, Andy, and Stephen had left. Andy ran back into the log house several times for things they remembered at the last minute. The last time was for the miner's pick and gold pan that belonged to his great Uncle Joe. Finally everything was packed, but before leaving, Stephen called them all together for a meeting on the porch.

"Now, I guess I don't have to tell you that I don't believe for one minute that this idea of murder is true," Stephen started.

"Dad!" Andy interjected.

"Let me finish," Stephen replied, raising his hand toward Andy. "Listen to what I have to say. Like I started to say, I don't really believe in the murders."

"Murders? Dad?" Andy broke in.

"No. Murder." Stephen answered. "Besides, we have no motive for any of this. However, I also believe that in this life it always pays to put the odds in your favor. So, Gary, I feel that just in case these wild ideas are right, you shouldn't check any more files for coded messages. Don't even run the program on your own computer. Someone could break into your house and discover what you have been doing. Even better, if you have a safe deposit box, copy all the important files to disks, put them in the box, and erase all traces from your computer. Above all, don't talk to anyone—even the police—about what you think. As for the rest of us, no word of any of this to anyone. We won't talk about this, at least in public. As far as anyone needs to know, we're just tourists on a trip. It might be better not to tell anyone about Uncle Joe either. I've taken one further precaution. Along with the copy of my will, I've added a complete description of your suspicions. If anything happens to all of us, at least someone will be able to know what you were thinking."

As the car was pulling out of the driveway, Andy suddenly asked Stephen to stop. "Dad, I want to tell Gary something about the computer model of Professor Greenly's."

"Gary," Andy called out of the car window. "I think I know why the tidal currents have been changing."

"Why?" Gary called back.

"It's something big! It's stuck in the channel! I think it's a pirate ship, dragged there by the strong currents. The weight of the gold in the hull would keep it on the bottom! I put a sunken ship into the channel and the currents suddenly matched the professor's new readings. Neat, huh?"

"Neat!" Gary called back, as Stephen's car accelerated out of the driveway. He didn't have the time to tell Andy that any pirate ship at the bottom of the channel would have, by now, been long turned to dust and carried away by the currents.

As they passed their gate, Jill turned to Karen and whispered, "Why did my Dad put a note in his will if he doesn't believe in any of this?"

"Beats me," Karen shrugged.

A strong, warm wind buffeted the car as it turned east, away from the suburbs, and began to climb into the foothills of the Cascade Mountains. Karen watched the Douglas fir trees bend westward under the steady wind. Small pieces of branches flew downward, blowing across the pavement in little swirls. Occasionally, larger gusts of wind reached down to shake the car, as warm air pushed its way into the open windows and over the passengers. The tops of the mountains were outlined against a thin strip of vivid blue sky. Gray clouds bordered the blue above. The clouds were thin at their eastern edge, but over Karen's head, they were thicker. Shafts of gray hung below the thicker clouds, their fingers reaching towards the car.

"What's making it so windy?" Karen asked, as another gust of wind cascaded from the tree tops and enveloped their car, and the warm wind blew her hair across her face. Karen glanced over at Stephen, remembering the warm winds of their dreams.

"I can tell you!" Andy broke in, before Stephen had a chance to reply. "It's Dad's lecture number 23."

Karen turned and leaned over the seat back in order to look at Andy. "What do you mean, lecture 23?" she asked.

"Dad has standard lectures he gives on practically every subject. After a while, Jill and I started to number them, for fun. Actually, we don't have all his lectures numbered. Well—actually, we use 23 as the number for all of them."

"So, Andy, let's hear lecture number 23," Karen said, turning back to watch the tall trees with their backs bent to the strong east wind, and the thin strip of blue sky over the mountains the car was climbing towards.

"It's all because of high pressure," he began. "High pressure east of the mountains we're climbing over, and low pressure. Low pressure on this side because a storm is coming inland from the Pacific Ocean. That's what the clouds overhead are from. The mountains block the air from blowing across from the high to low pressure."

"If the mountains block the wind, why is it blowing so hard?" Karen asked, as an especially hard gust hit the car pushing it over the center line into the next lane.

"Because," Andy continued, "the mountains block the air on the surface. The first place the air can finally blow westward is through the valleys that cut across below the peaks. Because all that air has been trapped, at the first chance it pushes westward, spilling down the western slopes."

"Can I tell Karen why the air is warm?" Jill interrupted.

"Sure honey," Stephen replied, glancing in the rear view mirror, and seeing the look on Andy's face. Andy started to object, but Stephen cut him off. "Andy, let Jill tell Karen some of the story."

"OK—" Jill started, anxious to show that she also knew something about the weather. "The wind is warm because it blows down the western slopes, like Andy said. As it blows down, the air pressure around it increases, squeezing it and making it hotter. It's like when you blow up a tire. The increased pressure in the tire causes the tire to warm up. That's right, isn't it Dad?"

"So far it's right, but do you know why the clouds seem to be reaching down towards the car, and why that thin strip of blue sky is right over the mountains?"

Jill paused as she glanced up at the strange clouds overhead. "The air—I think the air coming from the east is dry. Yeah, that's the reason. The dry air is evaporating clouds from the storm as it moves eastward. The hanging cloud above us is not really a cloud —it's—"

"Virga!" Andy interrupted his sister. "It's falling rain that's also evaporating in the dry air."

"Rain?" Stephen asked, glancing back in his mirror.

"Snow!" Jill quickly replied, satisfied that she had regained the stage from Andy. "Remember what Dad taught us, 'When it rains, it doesn't pour—it snows.' Like the commercial, but when it rains it almost always snows."

"It snows?" Karen asked puzzled. "How can it snow when it's raining, or not even raining, like now?"

"I forgot, but I can tell you now," Andy said, sensing his chance. "The temperature gets colder as it gets higher in the sky. Somewhere above us the temperature falls below freezing. If the clouds are higher than that, any precipitation that falls out of them will be snow. It melts into rain when it falls into warmer air. Even in summer—that's right, isn't it Dad? Even in summer, when it rains, it's snowing somewhere over us."

"For where we live, and for most of the United States, that's right," Stephen answered, turning the car away from the foothills to begin the steeper climb toward the crest of the pass. "Some places in the world, where it's warmer, the rain that hits the ground was never snow. That's called warm rain."

As the hills gave way to mountains, a rushing stream paralleled the road, then moved away into the tall trees. Bare areas carved into the sides of the mountains by repeated avalanches became prevalent. The air blowing into the car through the windows became cooler and smelled fresh, like the forests and mountains surrounding them. All of them found they were breathing more deeply, enjoying the change of air.

"Look to the right, Karen—in that clearing—just up from the road," Stephen pointed. "See where a road branches off into the woods?"

Karen looked, but couldn't see any difference in the forest. "I can't see anything there. Is it right where you're pointing?"

"Look again, there should be part of a road right to the side, then a clearing back from it."

"I don't see anything like that," Karen replied, searching the side of the road for any sign of what Stephen was talking about. "It just looks like unbroken forest to me."

Stephen became silent as he went back to driving. For a while they drove on, everyone waiting for him to speak. Finally, he turned back to Karen and his children. "I knew that someday all traces of what was there would vanish back into the forest. I—I just didn't think it would be so soon. When I was younger, before you kids were born, I studied snowfall for several winters in the mountains. Towards the last years of our project we needed additional sites where we could take snow measurements. I looked on both sides of the pass along the main highway, since side roads were not often plowed in winter. We weren't having much luck finding new locations, so on one trip in the fall I turned off at a small road leading into the woods. Back where I pointed. Now, the freeway passes it by, but then the turn-off from the main road was still usable.

"At the end of the road, hidden from the road by the forest, I spotted a cabin. It didn't look too large from the outside, and it was long and narrow, the long side facing the road. I got out of the truck and walked up to the only door. I knocked, and waited for what seemed like an awfully long time. I was just about to turn away when the door was opened by an elderly man. He was shorter than me, and the first thing I noticed was that he was wearing something like a smoking jacket. You know, like men wear after dinner, like what they wear in old 1930's movies. As he invited me in he shuffled along in old fashioned men's slippers. He led the way down a short hallway and into a long room that ran the whole length of the cabin. Windows covered the opposite

wall, giving a spectacular view of the valley and mountains beyond
the road. But it wasn't the view that really caught my eye, it was
the two large, old fashioned pump organs that were at either end
of the room. The woodwork was different on each of them, and
they had been well maintained over the years. After I talked about
the research project I was a part of, I couldn't resist asking about
the organs. We sat for over an hour, looking out at the view as he
told me the story.

"Before he retired, he was a pipe organ voicer. Each pipe on an
organ had to be tuned by hand, but they called what they did on
the pipes 'voicing', not tuning. I guess they considered the sound
more akin to the human voice since there was much more to the
quality of the sound than the actual pitch. Anyway, at the time he
was working, most good theaters had a pipe organ down in front.
Traveling concert organists would play at these theaters for large
audiences. Of course, this was before television. Only the best
voicers would work during a concert, and he was one of them.
They had to listen while the concert was going on for any pipes
that were going off tune, then in the midst of all the noise, crawl
back into the organ and re-voice the pipes. It's hard to believe, but
this was going on while the artist was playing.

"His wife also played the organ, so when he retired to that
cabin, he moved both his wife's and his organ into the front room.
In the evenings they played duets together, by themselves, in that
beautiful mountain setting.

"It turned out that his property was surrounded by too many
trees to be a good site for sampling, but I have never forgotten
him, or his house. The Forest Service planned to tear down the
cabin and close off the access when the old man died, or got too
old to stay there. Every time I drove up the pass after my visit, I
looked over to see if the cabin was still there. I like to think about

that old couple, together, playing the organs in that long room with the beautiful view. One time, the access was closed. Now all traces are gone—I—I—liked to think that I would someday spend my last years with someone I loved—like that—together—but . . ." Stephen's voice became deeper and trailed off.

Jill, Andy, and Karen stared out of the windows. Jill seemed especially quiet. As the car neared the summit of the pass, it passed under the remaining higher clouds, and broke into the sun. A cloudless blue sky stretched before them as the road turned downward, and the sun streaming through the windows seemed to bring them out of their somber moods.

"Are we going to sing that song, Dad, like we always do when we cross the Columbia River?" Jill asked, breaking the silence.

"What song is that?" Karen asked.

"Oh, 'Roll on Columbia' by Woody Guthrie," Stephen answered. "He wrote it during the Great Depression to commemorate the building of the Grand Coulee Dam. It's a family tradition. We always sing it any time we cross the river. You'll know when we're getting close. By that time the land is all dry and desert, and we start down a long decline. All of a sudden the river appears, deep and wide. It's a surprise to see all that water flowing in such a dry land. I can only imagine how surprised the first explorers were."

As the tall Douglas fir became sparser, and eventually gave way to pine, and the pine eventually gave way to sagebrush, Karen thought about Stephen. She wondered if he loved her outside of their lucid dreams they had together, like he did inside them. He's given me the greatest sex I've ever had, maybe anyone has ever had, she thought. So why am I not satisfied? What is wrong with me that I can't be satisfied with those dreams? Karen's thoughts turned to Jill and Andy. She was beginning to like them a lot, maybe too much. She found herself wishing she could be a part of this family. She wanted to help fill a void she felt in all of them. Or, she thought, is it a void I want to be there, so they will need me to fill it?

Andy's excited voice interrupted her thoughts.

"We're starting down towards the Columbia. Karen! Look! We'll see the river anytime. Keep watching. Don't start until we reach the bridge!"

Three voices began the familiar verse together. "Roll on Columbia, roll on. Roll on Columbia, roll on. Your power is turning our darkness to dawn. Roll on Columbia, roll on."

Karen joined in the second singing of the verse. She liked feeling a part of their family. As they finished a third chorus, the road turned northward along the tall banks that had been carved by the Columbia, and quickly rose upwards away from the river onto rolling, dry hills. Karen took a last backward look at the river as it retreated behind them.

When we sing this song again, she thought, will I be satisfied? Will I feel a real part of this family?

Before long, the sagebrush changed to golden fields of wheat, broken up by isolated patches of freshly plowed ground. Dust devils swirled across the dry earth, lifting brown clouds of dust skyward.

"Slow down! Slow down, Dad," Andy called out. "That big dust devil is coming across the road. Try to hit it!"

"I'll try," Stephen replied, slowing down and turning into the left lane toward the direction of the dust devil. The car was suddenly buffeted to the right, then to the left, as the tightly wound whirling wind moved across the highway.

"Wow, that was the best one ever!" Andy shouted.

"Hey, does anyone—?" Stephen started to ask.

"Angular momentum!" Jill and Andy chorused. "Conservation of angular momentum!"

"The hot air rises in small bubbles," Jill continued.

"Surrounding air rushes toward the rising bubble," Andy added.

"The surrounding air is slowly rotating," Jill broke in.

"As it comes together," Andy interjected.

"It spins faster, like a figure skater pulling in her arms," they both finished together.

"Lecture number—?" Karen asked.

"Twenty three."

The wheat fields stretched from horizon to horizon. Small groves of trees, sheltering the farmhouses, were lightly sprinkled amongst the wheat, spread out from each other by miles of waving gold. Andy and Jill had fallen asleep.

"It's the miles of wheat," Stephen remarked to Karen. "It never fails to put them to sleep. When they were smaller, I welcomed the break. Now, that they are older, they're better company. See that old, abandoned farmhouse on the side of the road? The one without any windows. See how weathered it is? It has turned the color of the fields. I wonder what its history was. Did a family live there? Was there the laughter of children inside its walls? Was there a man who loved a woman? Did he lay her down behind those walls, behind those empty window frames? Did he know how fleeting their happiness would be when he loved her? Houses like that always fill me with feelings of sadness tinged with gladness . . ." Stephen finished, his voice trailing off.

"I love looking at the wheat," Karen replied. "I wonder what it would be like to live in one of those houses, way out in the middle of nowhere, isolated from anyone, surrounded by acres of wheat blowing in the breeze." Karen glanced into the back seat to see if Andy and Jill were still fast asleep. "I'd like to walk naked into those fields. I'd like to feel the hot sun on my back, and the cool earth under my bare feet. I'd like to let the wind blow the stalks of wheat against me. I want the sun to turn me the golden color of the wheat. I want to walk so far that the farmhouse disappears, that I'm alone in a waving sea of gold. Might the heads of wheat caress me, like the tall stalks of grass in our first lucid dream, Stephen?" Karen asked.

"Sure, but won't the wheat be scratchy?" Stephen replied.

"I want soft caresses. Can you make them soft for me?"

"I can make them like the soft kisses of a cool breeze. Of course that will cost you extra," Stephen noted in a serious tone.

"Add it to my bill," Karen laughed.

"Would you like anything else? I'm having a special on ponds. I throw in colored fish at no extra charge, if they aren't the jumbo size."

"A pond would be nice. I'll take the colored fish. The small ones would be fine. The large ones are too inquisitive."

"What about flowers? The sale goes through this week on small purple ones. Would you like to try a different scent?"

"Oh, I couldn't change my scent! I love smelling it after our dreams. I'll never want to change it," Karen said, looking over at Stephen.

Suddenly, Stephen slowed the car and pulled onto the shoulder, so he could look over at Karen—into her eyes. "Karen, I'm so glad that you came with us," he said. "I'm glad you have come into my life."

"I'm glad, too, Stephen," Karen replied back, searching his eyes for a clue to his feelings. "I'm glad, too."

"How come we've stopped?" Jill asked in a sleepy voice. "Are we in Idaho?"

"Not yet, honey. I'm getting a little sleepy, so Karen is going to drive for a while."

Wheat fields gave way to scattered pines, and the scattered pines to forest as they climbed into the Rockies. Lake Coeur D'Alene passed behind them. Then, it was over the 4th of July Pass and down past the small towns of Cataldo, Pinehurst, Smelterville, Kellogg, and Wallace. Most were built on the backs of countless miners. Then, up the final barrier before Montana—Lookout Pass. When they reached the summit, Stephen asked Karen to pull to the side and stop.

"There it is kids, Montana! Everywhere you look it's Montana! You'll soon see why it's called the 'Big Sky Country'," Stephen added.

Taking over the driving from Karen, Stephen pulled back onto the freeway. "Well, Andy. Will you solve your mystery in Montana?" Stephen asked. Andy was too busy reading occasional signs along the road, advertising what sounded like a tourist trap, to answer.

"Dad, can we stop at the '$10,000 Silver Dollar Bar'?" Andy asked. "It sounds like fun."

Stephen looked at the time. "I guess so. I don't think we can get all the way to Butte tonight anyway. We can stop there for dinner."

"How far can we get tonight?" Karen asked.

"I figure we can make it to Deer Lodge, then Butte will be less than an hour's drive in the morning."

Andy became excited as the signs appeared more frequently. Finally, they passed the last billboard and turned under the freeway and into the parking lot. Suddenly, Andy became silent.

"Dad. I won't be able to see the 10,000 silver dollars set into the top of the bar. I'm too young," Andy said disappointedly.

"I guess that lets me out too," Jill added, slumping back into her seat.

"Oh," Stephen said laughing. "This is Montana. Children can

go into bars, as long as they don't drink. Now if you promise not to drink, too much that is—" Before Stephen could finish, Jill and Andy were out the back doors of the car and heading across the parking lot.

Karen took her time opening the car door. She was glad to have a moment alone with Stephen. "When they were asleep, did you mean it when you said you were glad I came along?" she asked him, turning to look directly at him.

"Yes, I meant it very much."

"Do you love me?"

"Yes."

"Can you love me the way a woman needs to be loved by a man?"

"I can't."

"Why?"

"I can't."

"Can you tell me why?"

"Maybe."

"Now?"

"No," Stephen said, sliding out the driver's door and turning away from Karen. "Don't be mad at me. You're the first person I've even felt I could tell. I just need some more time. Could you let me have that time?"

"Oh Steven,," Karen replied, "because I love you, and because love is patient, I can let you have that time."

Once inside the bar, Stephen and Karen found Andy carefully looking at all the souvenirs. Jill was staring at the examples of western art that lined the walls.

"See anything you like, honey?" Stephen asked.

"It's a mixed bag. There're some really nice pieces mixed in with some pretty garish examples. Like always, the ones I like are way over my budget," Jill replied, turning toward the bar. "Come see the bar. There really are 10,000 silver dollars in the bar, and poker machines, too."

During dinner, the couple sitting at the next table kept looking over at the piece of fool's gold Andy had purchased earlier. The man was tall and slim, and, judging by his weathered face, must have spent quite a bit of time outdoors. His wife was shorter, and didn't seem the outdoor type at all. His hands were rough from work, while hers looked soft with well shaped fingernails. Finally, the man leaned over toward Andy and asked. "That's a nice example of fool's gold you have there, son. Can I look at it?"

"Sure," Andy replied, handing the rock over to the man.

"I've seen plenty of this myself. If you folks are interested in ore, there's a nice mining exhibit in Butte, that is if you're going through there."

"That's where we're going," Andy replied. "My great uncle lived there."

"Actually, we're not sure if we're going to Butte," Stephen broke in. "This is our first time in Montana, and we haven't really decided what we want to see. I was thinking of going north to Great Falls. My daughter's interested in western art."

"Was it your uncle, or your wife's that lived in Butte?" he asked, looking over at Karen.

"It's my wife's," Stephen answered. "But he didn't live in Butte. He was a dry land farmer in eastern Montana—out in Glendive."

"Is that right, honey?" Stephen asked Karen, looking at her with steady eyes.

"Well, he didn't farm too long, and the family eventually lost track of him, but I think it was Glendive," Karen replied, looking at Stephen with a puzzled look.

"My wife and I are planning on spending several days in western Montana," the man said, as they rose to leave. "I'm a consultant for the company that's considering a joint venture with the mining exhibit I told you about. They might reopen the mine that's at the site."

"Is it a gold mine? Stephen asked.

"Yes, and quite famous too. It's called the Orphan Girl."

CHAPTER NINETEEN

WALLS WE BUILD

KAREN AND JILL walked side by side down the short main street of Deer Lodge. Stephen and Andy trailed behind. It was early and only a few stores were beginning to open. The lone stoplight was working away, oblivious to the lack of traffic to stop. The Montana dawn was all around them. The open fields of ranches started only a few blocks from where they walked. Beyond the fields came short grass prairie. The high prairie quickly turned into rolling hills, and the rolling hills into tall mountains. The tall mountains were surrounded everywhere by endless sky. Sky, mountains, hills, prairie, fields, with a tiny dot of a town in the middle. Stephen watched Andy slowly turn completely around as he took it all in.

"I know," Stephen said. "I know what you're feeling. Everywhere you stand in Montana, it feels like you're at the center, and around you is everything else in the world. It's the feeling that any direction you might go would go forever—that the whole world must be Montana. It's wonderful. Isn't it?"

"It's wonderful," Andy replied, still slowly turning.

"Hey," Jill called back. "If you keep doing that, people will think we're tourists."

"It's OK Andy," Stephen countered in a low voice. "We are tourists, and that's exactly what we want people to believe."

They continued toward the edge of town, walking past the wall of the old Montana State Prison which rose abruptly from the edge of the sidewalk.

"Stephen," Karen called, as she turned to look back. "The old prison is open today for self-guided tours."

"Dad!" Andy hollered, as he ran ahead to catch up with Jill and Karen. "There's also an old Ford car museum. We can see both. How about it?"

Stephen hurried to catch up with them. "What time does it open? In an hour? I wanted to get to Butte this morning, but it might be better if we didn't go right to Butte." He dropped his voice. "Yes. This might be better if we take some time here to see the sights. Anyone watching us won't be so suspicious if we act like we're in no hurry to get to Butte."

"Who's watching us?" Andy asked back, trying to match his dad's low voice, as he looked at the few people on the street. "I don't see anyone watching us."

"We don't really know anyone in this town, or in Montana for that matter," Stephen replied. "We don't know any of these people. Any one of them could not belong here, and we wouldn't know that until it was too late."

"What's this 'too late' stuff?" Karen asked, cupping her hands around her mouth, hunching over, mimicking Stephen's voice.

"It's like this, you rats," Jill added, drawing her finger across her throat in a slicing motion.

"Them that dies will be the lucky ones," Andy whispered.

"Them that dies will be the lucky ones?" Karen asked in her regular voice. "What does that mean?"

"It's from 'Treasure Island'," Jill explained. "Long John Silver says it to Jim. It's a family joke. It's our way of saying something isn't actually dangerous, that we're just having fun."

"Are we just having fun, Dad?" Andy asked, sounding disappointed.

"We should try to make everything fun, but, no Andy. Even though we're having fun, we don't really know what we're up against. It could be nothing." Stephen again lowered his voice, as he drew them closer around him. "It could be deadly. People have disappeared. They could be enjoying themselves somewhere, right as we speak, or—they could be—dead!" Stephen said, as he suddenly grabbed toward Andy, making Andy jump.

"Hey!" Karen said, finding she'd also inadvertently jumped backward. "Let's find somewhere to eat. I'd just as soon be pushing up daisies on a full stomach," she added, as they all turned, laughing, back toward the center of town.

After breakfast at the Broken Arrow the four "tourists" entered the old prison. Andy and Jill sauntered off towards the empty cells. Karen and Stephen walked out into the prison yard and stood in the middle of the enclosure. From there, they could see the tops of the surrounding hills and mountains. A warm wind blew Karen's hair from around her eyes. As she turned to let the sun fall directly on her face she spoke to Stephen. "How could the men sit here, surrounded by all this beauty, and know they couldn't go to it? How could they hear the sounds of everyday life in the town, right on the other side of the walls, and not go crazy? How could they have possibly tolerated it?"

"People adjust," Stephen replied. "They find other things to make themselves happy. We all surround ourselves with walls like these, and we adjust. Oh, I don't mean real solid walls like these, but they might as well be real. Maybe it's fear of something that builds the walls, or a past hurtful experience. Whatever. We stand in the middle of those walls, looking out at the town on the other side, wishing we could go there, but we're too afraid to let the walls fall down from around us." Stephen suddenly fell silent, staring out at the hills and mountains.

"Have you built any walls?" Karen quietly asked.

"Oh, I know what it's like to build those walls," Stephen said, still looking at the distant hills. "And I know that those walls we build might as well be as solid as these ones in this prison, and the wall surrounding me is higher and more solid than these."

"What wall, Stephen?"

"The wall that separates me from you. You're just inches from me, but there is a wall between us that is so high I can't climb it. But like I said, people adjust. They find other things to make them happy. It's OK. I watch you. I wish I could be like other men, and it hurts, but —it's OK."

"Could I break down that wall for you?"

"No. Only we can break down the walls we build."

"Where did your wall come from, that it's so strong?"

Stephen didn't answer her. He continued to stare into the distance.

"Stephen, let me help you."

"No one can."

"I want to, I love you."

"Don't believe it when you hear that love conquers all," Stephen said.

"Let me help you, let me try."

"I have to help myself."

"Can you?" asked Karen.

"Don't be sad. It's OK."

"Not for me."

"I've learned to live with it. Can you?"

"I don't know."

"Dad! Karen! We're done looking at the prison. Let's go into the gift shop," Jill called from a corner of the prison yard. "We're ready."

Karen and Jill walked together along the rows of the museum-type displays and racks of items for sale. Stephen liked to watch the two of them talking and laughing together. She needs Karen in her life, he thought. Not just a friend, but someone to always be around, to be there whenever she needs her. To be a part of our family. But can it happen? Will Karen take me as I am?

After making several small purchases at the gift shop, everyone walked over to the Ford Car Museum. Andy and Stephen especially enjoyed seeing the rows and rows of old cars gleaming under the overhead lights. Before long, though, they were on the road once again.

Andy was particularly interested in the nearly bare hills surrounding them as they drove towards Butte. A few trees grew in patches, but mostly the hills were only grass and a few low bushes. They stood out in stark contrast to more distant hills that seemed covered with trees.

"Why are these hills so bare?" Andy finally asked.

"Because of an animal," Stephen answered.

"What animal?"

"One that first cut down all the larger trees to make timbers to shore up the mine shafts. When the larger trees were cut, this animal smelted gold and copper ore out in the open, in large smoldering fires. The arsenic in that smoke killed all the smaller trees that weren't cut. It killed all the bushes and grass. Sometimes the smoke was so thick in Butte that it seemed more like night than day. It's ironic. The arsenic that men and women breathed made their skin pale white. At that time women with pale skin were considered real beauties. Butte women were considered the most beautiful of all, but they paid for that beauty with their lives."

"It's the same today," Jill interjected.

"How's that, honey?"

"Pale skin is out, but tanned skin is in. How many people will pay for that with their life?"

"At least they choose it themselves. Butte women didn't have any choice, except not to breathe. What choice is that?" Stephen asked.

Butte seemed surrounded with leftovers of its mining past. The old part of town was riddled underneath with miles of now unused mine shafts. This made the streets somewhat uneven and rolling. Above the ground, pieces of the frames that supported the large pulleys used to lower cars into the mines could be seen on several of the hills the town was built on. A large part of the original town had disappeared into an enormous open pit mine. When the higher grade ore in the deep shaft mines had played out, the lower grade ore could still be successfully mined by literally digging up the ground. Whole neighborhoods disappeared into the pit. Finally the low grade ore became too expensive to dig, and now all that was left was a giant man-made toxic lake, located far below ground level.

"Look at all the stained glass windows on the older houses," Jill remarked. "I've never seen so many. Could you slow down so I can get a better look. I wonder if I could buy a book telling about them?"

"I'm sure you can," Stephen said, slowing the car down so Jill could get a better look. "You can probably get one at the restored historic town and mining museum. It's funny that you noticed the stained glass windows. Butte does have more than most cities, and I guess it's an indication of the vast wealth taken out from under the town. But, if only a small part of that vast wealth had stayed here, Butte would be the most beautiful city in the world. The companies that owned the mines took most of the wealth back east, and left Butte looking like countless other western towns that didn't have such wealth buried beneath them. If there's a hell, it must be for men like that, and the crooked politicians that let it happen. Today, things would be different. Oh—there are still plenty of people willing to sell out their neighbor for a price, but citizens aren't so powerless now. If the same level of mining was taking place today, more would be kept—but, now the ore is played out."

Andy became more excited the closer they came to the entrance to the museum. As they pulled into the parking lot, he could see the towering gallus frame of the Orphan Girl Mine looming above the museum. Down to the left, the buildings of the historic town seemed small, compared to the gallus frame. The museum itself was built into the building that held the giant winches used to lower the cars into the mine. The Orphan Girl mine dominated the whole hilltop. Once a rich source of silver and zinc, the 3,200-foot deep, three-compartment mine had long ago been mined out.

"What's all the activity around the mine?" Karen asked.

Stephen was also curious. Men were up on the gallus frame making repairs to the structure. New pulleys were being fitted in place of the old ones. A temporary winch had been set up to lower a small cage into the mine which could hold a few men and some tools. The wooden cover, erected to cover the entrance to the old mine shafts, had been replaced with a new building. Several trucks were backed up to the work area, waiting to unload wood and materials. As the group walked toward the entrance of the museum, a cement truck drove through the gate into the museum area, replacing one that had just pulled out.

"Remember," Stephen warned them, "act like any tourist would, but be on the lookout for anything that might give us a clue as to what might be going on."

"What's all the activity around the old mine?" Stephen asked the woman seated behind the counter where the brochures were stacked. She was older, like many people who filled unpaid positions out of a sense of duty to the community. Her hair was done up in a neat gray braid pinned on top of her head and she had a well-worn gray sweater draped over her shoulders. She had looked bored sitting behind the counter when they walked in, but she brightened up with Stephen's question.

"It's something that will be wonderful for the museum," she began. "Not right now, but in a year it will be. A company, the Living History Company, is going to reopen the mine. But, not only the mine. They're going to turn the whole complex into what is called a living history display. Like Williamsburg, back east. The historic buildings will be opened up with people in them dressed in period clothes. They'll bake bread, and do lots of other things too, but the mine will be the centerpiece. They will operate it like a real mine was operated at the turn of the century for five days a week."

"Like an actual working mine?" Stephen queried.

"Not exactly like a real working mine since they won't take out much ore. Just enough to make it look like the real thing."

"Will people be able to go down into the mine?" Andy asked excitedly.

"That hasn't been decided, but the company and all of us at the museum hope that some access can be provided for visitors."

"Isn't all this construction costing a lot of money?" Stephen wondered aloud. "I wouldn't think that there was a lot of money in this type of thing."

"The company has been blessed with a large grant from some very rich individuals, I understand. This will make it possible to run it without charging too much for admission. Of course it won't be free, like it is now. It's too bad that you're here now, before it's open. But, come back in a year."

"It looks like there's lots to see today. I don't think we'll be disappointed. Thank you for being so helpful," Stephen said, as they made their way into the museum.

Jill and Karen paired up, as did Andy and Stephen. The top floor of the museum was dominated by the giant winches that powered the cars in and out of the mine. These were the original winches, and they didn't appear to be undergoing any repairs. "Maybe," Stephen mused, "they'll build other winches outside of the museum building and leave these alone."

It took a lot of time to go through the museum. Many of the displays dealt with the Orphan Girl and other mines. There was a miniature working model of the mine. In addition, there was a substantial exhibit on the cultural life of Butte at the time the mine was open, including a full bar from the oldest tavern in town.

"I wonder if my uncle stood at this bar?" Stephen asked as he and Andy rested one foot on the brass railing that ran along the bottom. Stephen ran his hand along the polished top, lost in his own thoughts. "Do you think this bar has any secrets we need to know?" he asked Andy in a low voice. "If it does, we'll probably never know them."

Three hours later the two groups met back at the entrance. Everyone was tired from looking at all the exhibits. When they got outside, Stephen drew them over to the side, away from the other visitors and the workers. "Let's go into the historic town. We can talk there, as long as other people aren't too close by," he told them.

Hell Roarin' Gulch, as the historic town was called, was a collection of historic buildings trucked in from surrounding areas, and assembled into what a mining town might have looked like at the turn of the century. What set it apart from other historic towns was the emphasis on mining. Several of the old buildings, including the Assay Office, owed their existence to it. Although only tourists roamed the streets, Stephen could see why the woman behind the desk was excited about having it run as a real working town. Now, it was more like a ghost town, but a working town with period workers and residences could bring it to life.

The foursome walked slowly past the time-worn buildings. Their old boards contrasted with the boardwalk under their feet that was made with modern, treated lumber. Andy stopped to look into several of the buildings.

"Hey, Dad," Andy called. "Look here! It's a piece of mining machinery. It says it was developed by an engineer that worked at the mine, Joe Macky."

"Joe Macky!" Stephen replied, moving closer to Andy so he could see in the building. "Joe Macky. I'm sure it's my uncle. He did work at this mine. What's it say about him?"

"Not much. Only that this drill bit sharpener was developed by him, and it made it possible to use an improved drill for mining which greatly increased the daily output."

Turning away, they continued walking down the street. When they came to the end of the boardwalk, instead of turning the corner Stephen led them out towards some old mining cars that were standing on a short section of track.

"We can talk here," Stephen said in a lower than normal voice. "Did anyone see anything that might give us any clues as to how this mine might tie in to the disappearances? Andy and I looked at everything, but didn't come up with any ideas."

"Everything looked normal to us, too," Karen remarked. "Jill and I looked at some of the exhibits twice, but we didn't see anything that gave us any ideas, either."

"Well, maybe we're dead in the water. We could look around outside some more, but I doubt we'll find anything."

"Phooey!" Andy sighed, leaning against Stephen. "Can't we stay just a little longer? I thought we'd for sure find something."

"OK, let's give it one more try," Stephen said, putting his arm around Andy's shoulders. "Think! Did anyone see anything that was different from the normal exhibits?"

"What do you mean by different?" Jill asked.

"It's hard to know what I mean. I don't even have any idea how there might be a connection from here to our city, or even if any of Karen's and Gary's suspicions are correct, or what we might be looking for. What about anything that didn't seem to fit in, for lack of a better place to start."

They leaned back against the mining cars, all trying to remember anything that didn't seem to fit in with the exhibits. After several minutes of silence Stephen spoke up. "OK, now let's try thinking about anything that might have been recently moved or changed."

"Maybe," Jill started to speak, then stopped.

"What is it, honey?"

"Well—I don't know if it's anything or not."

"Go ahead," Karen added. "Any idea is worth thinking about."

"Well, you know how I like artistic things. I wasn't really as interested in the objects in the different exhibits as I was in the way they were arranged. Whoever had put the exhibits together was quite good, but one exhibit caught my eye. It was the samples of minerals found in the Orphan Girl Mine. They were displayed in a pattern like a wagon wheel, but part of a spoke was missing. I could see where the rock samples had been since light had faded the paint on the board they rested on. They left a dark shadow where they had been. I remember thinking that I wouldn't have left it like that, but would have filled it in with something else, or perhaps changed the design."

"I remember looking at that, too," Stephen replied. "But I didn't think anything about it. Now that you mention it, it is a little strange. It might be something, or it might be nothing."

"What do you mean, Dad?" Andy asked, hopeful that Jill might have found something.

"Well, maybe someone wanted those particular samples for some reason, or maybe someone didn't want those samples seen, or maybe—well—for lots of reasons, probably all legitimate. But, if the board had faded around them, they must have been taken out long after they became a part of the exhibit. It's our only lead so we might as well pursue it. Let's go back inside, look at the ore samples again, and I'll talk to the lady behind the counter. We'll split up, like before. Don't go right to the ore samples. Walk around the others also. Let's meet back at the counter in about twenty minutes."

"So you're back for some more history," the woman behind the counter remarked as they all stepped back into the museum. "Didn't you get enough the first time? I've never seen a family spend so much time in here. It's nice to see children interested in the past."

"Well," Stephen replied. "I came through with my son, and my daughter came through with our friend. Now my daughter wants to show me some things she saw and Andy wants to show Karen the miniature mine model. We won't be too long."

"Take all the time you want. We're open for a couple more hours."

"Thanks."

Jill and Stephen pretended to look at several of the exhibits on the way to the ore display. Karen and Andy walked the opposite way, and all four of them found themselves meeting at the ore display case. They didn't speak, but silently looked down at the rock samples laid together to form the shape of a wagon wheel. Eight eyes lingered for a minute on the dark blue shadows where several rocks had been removed from one of the spokes. Then they split up again, making their way back towards the main counter.

"Well, I guess we've seen everything," Stephen said to the woman behind the desk. "Oh, there is something you can help me with, if you don't mind. My daughter is taking design classes at school. She was especially impressed with the design of the exhibits. Would it be possible to talk with the person who set up the exhibits? One of her assignments for next year will be to interview a designer, and this would be good practice for her."

"Sure, but these exhibits were set up in the early 60's. One person lives here in town who helped put them together. Her name is Martha Collins, and she lives out in the Flats."

"The Flats?"

"The new sections built on the level ground below the hills of the original city. I'll write her number down for you. She's getting older so you'll find her home on most nights."

"Thanks," Stephen replied. "We really appreciate your help."

"Come back again."

"We will."

CHAPTER TWENTY

WAGON WHEEL

"HELLO, MARTHA COLLINS? My name is Jill. I toured the mining museum today and I was very impressed with the way the displays were put together. I'm studying design in school, and I need to talk to designers for a project that I'll have next year. The woman at the mining museum gave me your name and said that you might be able to talk with me. Oh no. I was impressed with the displays and I would like to talk to you. I'm here with my father, brother, and a family friend. No, we don't. Yes, we could come tonight, and that might be better for us since we'll be leaving Butte soon. Yes, we will. I'll let you tell my father the directions."

The area called the Flats was much different than the older part of town. The older part was unique since it was built around the mines, both above and below ground. It was like no other town in the States. The newer homes built out on the Flats could have been part of lots of small towns built in the 40's, 50's, and 60's. The group pulled up in front of a modest one-story house, whose original siding had been covered over by the more modern aluminum type. The siding gave the house a neat, well-kept look. A small vegetable garden occupied much of the front yard. The front fence had been painted to match the siding. Stephen knocked on the front door. A short, gray-haired woman opened it for them.

"Hello, you must be Jill's family. Come in. It's nice to have some company in the evening. I don't get out much any more at night. We can sit in the front room. Your father can sit in the chair my husband used. Men seem to like it."

Jill, Andy, and Karen sat on the couch, facing Martha. "Now that we're settled, what can I do for you? I find it hard to believe that you're interested in the work of an old lady, but I'll help you all I can."

"You could start by telling me how the idea for the exhibits came about," Jill began.

"Well, my husband worked in the mines as a young man, then moved to the open pit when the deep shafts closed. He had always worried that the history of the deep mines and the life of the miners would be lost to the next generations. When he retired, we got together with several other mining couples and started a group concerned with finding and preserving all the remnants of the mining past. We started slowly at first, scouring garage sales and back yards for anything we could find. We collected it in old Sam Jones's barn. He was the fifth of eight Jones boys. All miners. He married a Burly girl. Nice family, the Burlys. All the Burly girls married miners, and they kept their houses neat as pins. Some families are just nice. Have you noticed that?"

"You're right, some families are just nice," Karen agreed, glancing over at Stephen and his children.

"After a while, word of mouth got around. People started bringing us whatever they had that might fit into our collection. Some of the pieces of mining equipment were quite large. We sold what we didn't want to keep, and used the money to buy other things we wanted."

"How did you get the Orphan Girl Mine for your site?" Stephen asked.

"Oh, we seriously collected for several years. Mary Gibbons, one member of our group, used to date a fellow in high school who went quite high in the Anaconda Company. He was a Smith. All the Smith boys were ambitious, and none of them very good looking either. That seems to run in families, too. Funny thing about the Smith boys. All married lookers. I guess ambition counted for something. At the fifty-year reunion of their class they got to talking about our group. He was interested, and he was staying the week, so we took him out to Sam's barn the next day. Since he grew up in Butte, I guess he wanted to help out his old town, and he was impressed with how much we had collected on our own. A couple of weeks later he called and said that the company would donate the old Orphan Girl Mine and surrounding property for a museum. The company couldn't donate it to us, since we weren't anything official, so we worked with the city government to form a non-profit organization. Having the mine site really helped increase the number of cash contributions. Of course, the non-profit status made any donations tax deductible."

"How did you come to do the exhibits?" Jill asked.

"Even though we started to bring in more money," Martha replied, "we needed most of the donations for the museum building and display cases. We couldn't afford to hire any expensive designer so the job fell to me since I had taught high school art classes for years. At first I was nervous and didn't want to have all that responsibility. But after I designed the first display, I found I had a talent for it. I had lots of help from our original group, too, and we felt our way along. I guess we did all right for small town people."

179

"Your design work would be very nice in a town of any size," Jill said. "How did you decide what to put in what displays?"

"We had collected lots of different things, and at first we were going to put like things together. Musical instruments in one case, for instance. Then we decided it might be more interesting to have display cases around common themes that might contain many disparate items."

"You mean, like the case built around family life—the one that contains musical instruments, but also examples of home remedies?"

"Actually, I've forgotten about some of the details. It's been quite a few years since we put some of the displays together. I have a scrapbook of pictures of all the displays. We could look at that, if you want, that is."

"Sure, that will make it easier to talk about the exhibits," Karen added, glancing over at Stephen.

While Martha was out of the room looking for the scrapbook, Stephen looked at each one of them in turn, silently putting his finger up to his lips.

"Here it is," Martha said as she returned. "Come, Jill, sit next to me on the couch. Anyone interested can gather here also. Let's see, the family life display is here somewhere."

For about an hour Jill and Martha discussed the artistic designs of the various displays. Andy was getting restless, as Stephen and Karen had begun talking between themselves.

"Oh, we've gone on long enough," Martha suddenly said, closing the book. "Maybe we can interest your brother in some homemade ice cream. I thought you might like to see how it was made in the old days. Do you think you're strong enough to crank the handle? All right then, come with me. I've already made the sauce, it just has to be frozen."

When Jill and Andy went out into the kitchen to help Martha prepare the ice cream, Stephen and Karen stayed behind in the front room. Stephen casually picked up the scrapbook and started to thumb through the pages. He recognized the displays from the day's visit to the museum, but was getting to the end of the book and still hadn't seen the picture of the ore display. One page was left, and Karen reached over to turn it for him. They both looked down at the page. The picture showed the display of the samples that came from the Orphan Girl Mine. They looked closer. The wagon wheel of ore was complete. Karen looked over at Stephen for his reaction, but he sat there motionless, staring at the picture. He slid Karen's hand off of the page and closed the scrapbook.

"Let's see if the ice cream is ready. Thinking about it is making me hungry," Stephen remarked, standing up from the couch, and quickly walking into the kitchen.

The kitchen table was small, but they squeezed around it, the home made ice cream sitting in the middle in a large bowl. They all, including Martha, helped themselves to several helpings. The ice cream was yellow and rich from all the egg yolks that went into it. "I use real cream, not milk, in my ice cream," Martha remarked.

"It's wonderful," Stephen said between mouthfuls. "Nothing beats cream and eggs for making real ice cream. Now it's going to be hard to go back to regular ice cream. Oh, by the way, I really enjoyed looking through your scrapbook. I was surprised at all the different kinds of rocks in the wagon wheel display. Did your husband collect them?"

"No. My husband worked at the Con, that is, Mt. Con. We wanted to display rocks from the Orphan Girl so we asked the father of one of the members of our group, Letty Harris's father, old Mick Jones. He had quite a collection from the Orphan Girl, and since I didn't know much about ore, he helped me put the

display together. It was sad that he didn't get to see the finished
display."

"What happened to him?" Jill asked.

"He was really enjoying the whole idea of the museum, but he
died in his sleep before it was completed. We were all pretty broken up over it. We only needed a few more rocks to finish the
spokes of the wagon wheel. Letty looked through her father's
things and brought over a box of rocks she found. I wasn't sure
what to pick, so I just took some that seemed interesting. We never
checked to see what they were, but it didn't seem to matter at the
time. We were more concerned with finishing the display and
putting her father's death behind us."

"Do you remember what the rocks looked like that you took
from the box?" queried Stephen.

"Oh no, not after all these years. I remember that they were a
part of a spoke. That's all. Just a part of one of the spokes."

"Would you know what happened to the other rocks?"

"No, I don't, but you could ask Letty."

"She's still alive?"

"She's alive all right. She lives in Wise River. Once a month we
get together at her house to play cards. One of my friend's sons
drives us there. Wise River doesn't have many houses. Her house is
the only log one. She's like me these days, always home. Why don't
I call her now? She'll enjoy the visit."

"We'd like to visit with her tomorrow afternoon, if that suits
her. We have some errands to run in the morning."

Martha set the phone down. "Its fine for tomorrow afternoon.
It's about an hour's drive from Butte."

They all thanked Martha for her hospitality as they stood to say
final good-byes on the front door step. "Oh Martha, could you do
me one last favor?" Stephen asked. "We met a couple whose

daughter is interested in design. They said they might visit the museum. Jill would like to contact her, but we lost her number. If anyone comes to ask you about our visit, could you give me a collect call at this number? It's our home phone."

Outside, Karen glanced over at Stephen with a puzzled look. "What's the deal with the phone number and why are you anxious to talk to her friend, Letty?"

"It's the rocks that are missing out of the display. They look like the one that my uncle had wrapped in the paper Andy showed you at home. Maybe there is something actually going on. I have an idea, but I don't want to tell you until I confirm something in the morning."

"Confirm what?" Andy broke in.

"We're going to pay a visit to the Montana Technical School of Mines."

"For what?"

"Let's just say I'm awfully glad you remembered to bring the box with Joe's gold pan and pick."

"Why?" wondered Andy.

"You'll see."

When they arrived at the motel, Stephen lifted the box containing the gold pan and pick from the trunk of the car. He brought the box into the motel and set it under the desk lamp. Reaching in, he took out the gold pan and the pick. Setting those aside, he reached back in, bringing out a small rock wrapped in old paper. Stephen carefully unwrapped the rock and held it under the light. He turned it around in his hand. Everyone stared at him in silence. Stephen stood up away from the lamp, and turned towards them. Three times he raised the rock over his head, each time silently mouthing the same words. Then he looked at each of them in turn. His eyes seemed to bore into theirs. Karen felt goose bumps rise on her shoulders and arms. He then kissed the rock, carefully wrapped it back up in the yellowed paper, and put it back in the box. He slowly closed the lid. He set the box high atop a shelf, leaving the pick and pan on the desk.

"Dad?" Jill asked.

"What?"

"Stephen?" questioned Karen.

"Tomorrow."

Tomorrow couldn't come fast enough for Karen. She tossed and turned most of the night. Her dreams were strange. She kept seeing Stephen lifting up the rock, then she was plunging into a mine shaft. Martha was calling after her, but she didn't look the same. She had long slender fingers and was dressed all in black. She held a small bird in her hand. Its neck was broken. She held it so its head fell back over her fingers. Karen couldn't stop falling. Martha was calling something, something about beauty—and death. Suddenly, Karen was in Martha's hands. Her head was bent back and Martha was stroking her hair with those long fingers. Karen couldn't feel anything below her neck. She tried to move her own fingers but couldn't. She opened her mouth to scream, but nothing came out. Martha's face turned into a man's face. He placed his fingers over Karen's eyes. He slowly closed her eyelids as fear swept through Karen. Her mouth had a bitter taste.

"My neck—he's broken my neck—help—help—!"

"Karen! Karen!" Jill said, shaking Karen awake. "What's the matter? You're white as a sheet. Were you dreaming?"

"Oh Jill! It was horrible—Martha—only it wasn't Martha -- turned into a man with long slender fingers. He—he was dressed all in black.—He broke my neck—but I wasn't dead.—He tried to close my eyes—his fingers—his fingers kept stroking my hair—I couldn't move."

Jill felt chills rise from her shoulders, up the back of her neck. "Was he short, and—and his fingers long and slender? Was he creepy, like an old-fashioned undertaker?"

"Yes—very creepy, sinister—almost like he enjoyed death."

"Oh, Karen," Jill said, moving closer to her in the bed. "Andy and I met a man just like that. It was at the Gallery Walk that Dad took us to. It was at an exhibit showing paintings that had a common theme of death. He gave me such a bad case of the shivers that I couldn't warm up until I got home in bed."

"Oh!" Karen bolted upright. "I saw the same man down by the water at the University. He startled Gary and me. We were talking about our suspicions concerning the coded messages on the computer. He—oh—he was holding a dead bird—like he was holding me in my dream—and stroking it—."

"Hold me, Karen," Jill pleaded. "I feel all cold inside. I'm scared, Karen. Will he hurt us?"

"No, he's only a man we don't know—a scary man—but just a man. He has no reason to hurt us."

"Then why am I so scared?"

"Sometimes dreams scare us—but they can't hurt us. They are what they are—only dreams, that's all." Only dreams? Karen thought, hugging Jill closer. Only—dreams can hurt you if they make you want something you can't have.

"Hey, wake up!. Time to get going. We have an appointment at 10. We can't be late!" Stephen announced, shaking their bed.

The Montana School of Mines was located on another hill in Butte, not far from the Mining Museum.

"Dad, why did anyone build a school here?" Jill asked. "It's a long way from anywhere, and Butte's so small."

"The School of Mines is one of the most prestigious. Students come from all over the world to study there. I guess, honey, it's only fitting that the city that took so much from the miners eventually repay that debt. Only that debt can never be repaid to the original miners. But, now other people have the opportunity to improve themselves at the school. Sometimes life is strange."

"What do you mean, Dad?"

"Wrongs are righted, but not always as fast as we would like."

"Who are we going to see?" Andy broke in. "Is it someone you know?"

"His name is Joseph Greeg. I haven't met him in person. I've only talked to him over the phone. A couple of years ago he needed some weather information in New Mexico for a mining project he was a consultant for. I spent a week, off and on, helping him. Now he's agreed to do a favor for us."

Joseph looked the part of a mining engineer. He was short and stocky, and wore khaki colored pants and shirt. His face was weathered from time outdoors, and a thick miner's mustache bristled out from under his nose.

"Stephen!" Joseph exclaimed, firmly shaking Stephen's hand. "Who're these fine looking people with you?"

"This is my daughter, Jill, my son, Andy, and our friend, Karen. We're being tourists. We were curious to see where my uncle lived, and I always wanted to show the kids Montana."

"Your uncle?"

"Yes, Joe Macky. He was an engineer at the Orphan Girl Mine."

"The Joe Macky?"

"I guess."

"If it's the Joe Macky I'm thinking about, he's quite famous. He invented a device to automatically sharpen the new type mining drill, among other inventions. I didn't know he was your uncle. Our students learn about him in our history of mining class. Have you been to see the Orphan Girl?"

"Yes, we toured the Mining Museum yesterday. It's amazing what they're doing to the old mine."

"We're pretty excited about it here. If they open part of it to the public, then we can show the students how deep shaft mining was done, and the conditions the miners had to endure. Well, what can I do for you today?"

Stephen reached into his pocket and brought out the rock that had been wrapped in the old yellow paper. "We need help in identifying this rock. Do you know what kind it is?"

Joseph looked closely at the rock. He took a plate made of what looked like dull porcelain and rubbed the rock rapidly across it. Then he looked at the streak under an eye piece. "I'm not sure," he said, raising his head to look at them. "Can I make a section of it, so I can look more carefully at the structure? I'll just cut a small piece from it."

Joseph led them into a large lab. He set the rock into a holder, then deftly cut a small piece from the corner with a special saw. He washed off the cutting solution and put the piece under a projection microscope, then stepped back and looked at the projected image on the screen. They all looked on in silence as Joseph studied the screen, occasionally pulling on his mustache. Finally, he went to a bookshelf, pulled out a large book, and began thumbing through the pages.

"I think I've found it," he said, looking back at the screen. "But, it's confusing. Are you familiar with the rare earths?"

"Somewhat."

"Rare earth elements have atomic numbers between 57 and 71. Oxides of rare earth elements are called rare earths. Of the over 1,500 mineral species, very few are rare earths. Samarskite is one of them, and can contain several of the rare earth elements. I'm certain this is samarskite. But notice the odd play of colors in the interior. Well, you wouldn't notice anything odd here, but it is rather unique to see such colors in samarskite. I'd have to do further chemical tests in the lab to be completely sure, but I think that this sample of samarskite contains extremely large amounts of the rare earth element lutetium."

"Lutetium?"

"Yes, lutetium. Where did you get this sample?"

"It was in some things my Uncle Joe had," Stephen answered. "Is it valuable?"

"Not really," Joseph replied. "A natural isotope is used to determine the age of meteorites, but there aren't any commercial uses for lutetium that I know of. I doubt if your uncle knew what was in this rock, and it certainly didn't look like any mineral that he would have known about or thought had any value. That's why you got it."

"But you said it was unique," Andy spoke up.

"Well, unique in that this rock contains very large amounts of lutetium. If lutetium was good for anything, ore like this sample would be very valuable, but now it's just a scientific curiosity. Would you mind if I kept the small sample for further testing, just to confirm my guess?"

"Well, that was a dead end," Andy remarked kicking at the dirt as they headed toward their car. "I was afraid the rock wouldn't be important."

"Don't bet on it," Stephen said, pulling the rock from his pocket, and holding it up in front of them. "Don't bet on it."

CHAPTER TWENTY-ONE

WISE RIVER

STEPHEN TURNED THE CAR south from Butte toward the town of Divide. At Divide he turned west into the mountains toward the town of Wise River. Everyone was curious to know what was so important about a rock that had no value, but Stephen wouldn't answer any of their questions.

"Dad, why are we going to talk to Letty Harris?" Andy asked for the fifth time since they left Butte.

"Do you think my Uncle Joe drove up these roads?" Stephen asked in return. "He had an old Model A Ford that he mounted an extra transmission in. That way he had multiple gears for traveling off the main roads. That old Ford could climb anything. I guess he had mines way up in the hills on roads so steep ordinary cars couldn't manage."

"Dad!"

"Yep. I sure wonder if old Joe came up this same road."

"Dad!!!"

"When he drove up here do you think he thought about the fact that his nephew would be driving up the same road 50 years later? Hey, here's the town."

Letty Harris's house wasn't hard to find. There weren't many houses in the town of Wise River. Only one was made out of logs, large, rough cut logs that were assembled before modern log-building techniques began to produce uniform shapes. The very bulk of the logs gave the house a look of permanence and set it apart from the few remaining homes. Old, but well kept, were the very words Stephen thought of when he turned into Letty's front yard. Before they had even opened the car doors, a tall, white-haired woman came walking briskly down the front walk. She had her soft white hair piled on top of her head in an old-fashioned bun, and when she bent over to open the back door of the car, Karen was struck by how pretty her blue eyes were.

"Hi. I'm Letty Harris. Martha called to say you'd be coming around in the afternoon. Let me help with that door. So, what are you doing in Wise River?"

"We're here to learn more about your father, Mick Jones," Jill answered. "Dad's curious about some rocks he had, but better let him tell you. He won't tell us what he's thinking."

"A mystery. Well, there's nothing like a mystery to make people thirsty. Come on up to the porch. There's a cool breeze blowing and I've squeezed some fresh lemonade."

Letty had already set out four glasses for them and one for herself. Andy noted, with satisfaction, the large plate of Oreos sitting on the table. Not the regular kind, but the double-stuffed ones. The pitcher of lemonade was placed in the center of the table. Real lemons floated in-between large chunks of ice. Little streams of condensation dripped down the outside of the pitcher onto the table. Stephen dipped his fingers in the water and brought his fingers back to touch his forehead.

"Tell us about your father," Stephen said, after everyone had settled back with a cold glass of lemonade and several cookies.

"What made him become a miner?"

"My mother. She was a mail order bride. She answered an advertisement back in Italy asking for single women to write to men who were looking for wives in Butte. She started to correspond with the owner of one of the hotels in town. He had plenty of money, at least compared to the average miner here. One thing led to another, eventually she agreed to come to Butte and marry him. He sent her the money for passage. Her arrival in town caused quite a stir. She was quite a looker in her younger days. Well, it turned out that when she met the man she was supposed to marry, she didn't like him. Of course he was plenty mad, and insisted she pay back all of the money he had sent for her passage. A clerk working in the hotel felt sorry for her and lent her the money to repay the owner of the hotel. His name was Mick Jones. You can guess what happened. They fell in love, and there wasn't any way he could keep his job at the hotel so he found a job in the mines."

"Did they live in Butte?" Karen asked.

"No. My father spent six days a week underground. He wanted to live somewhere away from the mines and to raise his family away from the smoke of the smelters. He boarded in town, and came home on Sunday."

"Home?" wondered Karen.

"Here. To this house in Wise River. My father built it. I've lived here since I was born."

"I can see why he wanted to live here," Stephen remarked, looking beyond the porch to the rushing stream and out to the forested mountains. For a few minutes Letty fell silent as they all gazed at the mountains.

"Would anyone like a refill on lemonade?" she finally asked, bringing her attention back to her guests. "I hope I'm not boring you folks. I'm enjoying telling the old stories."

"Not at all," Karen replied. "It's romantic—I like romance," she said glancing at Stephen. "But, how did you happen to stay in this house?"

"When I was first married I lived in Deer Lodge. My husband worked at the old prison. When my mother died, we moved in here to take care of Dad. After my husband passed, I couldn't think of any place else I would want to be. Someday I'll join my husband and parents over there." Letty pointed to the small graveyard behind the house. "But I've plenty of life left in me for now. So, what's this mystery about the rocks?"

"It's something to do with Dad's uncle, Joe Macky," Jill started to explain, but Letty cut her off.

"Old Joe Macky? My, my! They say it's a small world! By golly, old Joe Macky. I've haven't heard that name for years."

"Did you know him?" Jill asked.

"Know him? Why—he sat right here on this porch many a time. Right in that rocking chair your dad's sitting in. He and my father were good friends. They used to prospect together on Sundays. When they got too old to work they sat on this porch and talked. Oh, how I loved to hear the old stories they told. If I close my eyes I can still see them. So many stories about so many people. All gone now. All gone but the stories. So he's your uncle. I remember him when I was a little girl. He used to make a face on the end of his cut-off finger. He was quite a character. Wore long underwear winter and summer, and chewed his whole life. He used to spit in a can Dad kept on this porch. He could fix anything made by the hands of man. He kept Dad's old car running for years. I don't think there was anything he couldn't turn his hand to."

"They prospected together?" Stephen asked.

Letty started to answer but was interrupted by loud banging noises from around back of the log house. "Darn squirrels. They're back climbing on the rain gauge. They'll break it yet!" Letty exclaimed, reaching for an old broom leaning against the door frame. "This will scare them."

They trailed behind her as she charged off the porch and around into the back yard. "Get outta here, you red-haired pests," she yelled, swinging her broom at the fleeing squirrels. "That'll keep them away for awhile!" she said, still brandishing the broom.

"You're a cooperative observer?" Stephen asked, bending down closer to look at the rain gauge. "This is the old type. Didn't it ever get replaced?"

"They wanted to replace it about ten years ago, but I didn't want the new style. This old copper one has done all right. Besides, it was built from copper taken out from Butte."

"Have you been an observer long?"

"All my adult life. I took over from my Dad when he got too old to get out behind the house. I'm pretty proud of it. Between Dad and me, we've kept records at Wise River for over eighty years. Eighty-six to be exact. Eighty-six this very year. How do you know about these gauges?"

"Dad does research on weather at a university," Jill answered before Stephen could reply. "Karen works with him."

"Hey, Dad," Andy broke in. "Doesn't the paper the rock is wrapped in say something about rain gauges?"

"Let's see," Stephen said, taking the rock out of his pocket and carefully unwrapping the yellowed paper. "It reads, 'Missouri Hydrologic Bulletin. Daily Precipitation Station Changes. Wise River, Montana, moved one quarter mile NE of former location on August 18, 1927. No changes in Lat. or Long. or station name.'"

"Nineteen twenty- seven—I was ten then," Letty said as she

leaned on the broom. "I remember now. Dad and Joe staked a claim close to the original location of the gauge. Dad petitioned to have the gauge moved, just in case the claim amounted to anything. He loaded me and the gauge into a cart and he and Joe pulled both of us back here. My, that was so long ago. I can still feel the wind as it blew my pigtails, and how bumpy the ground was."

"This claim. Did it ever amount to much?" Stephen inquired.

"No. They dug off and on there for years, but never did find a vein below the surface. I guess they had found some surface ore that was promising, but that was it. By the time I was married, they had given up on it."

"Did this rock come out of that claim?" Stephen asked, showing Letty the rock that was wrapped in the Missouri Hydrologic Bulletin.

Letty took the rock in her hand and looked at it carefully. "I don't know, but I think I can find out," she said. "Let's go inside."

Letty led the way into the house, and into a small room in the back. "This was my Dad's room when we took care of him. I pretty much left everything just as it was when he died, except I gave away some of his clothes. Dad always kept good records of all his claims." Letty reached up and pulled down a dusty log book from a shelf. "Mick Jones, Claim Log," she read, rubbing the dust off the letters with her sleeve. She began to thumb through the old pages. "Here's a log for the Rain Gauge Mine, Wise River, Montana. I'm sure that's it. They didn't have any other claims in Wise River. Let's see. First found promising ore on June 22, 1926—see sample 22WR. Here's a copy of the assay report taped on the page. The ore looked very promising—hmmm—more entries about the ore. Here's one dated April 29, 1938—can't find the vein below the surface. More entries. May 3, 1943—can't find the vein, but keep finding rocks like samples 30WR-42WR. Here's the last entry. It's dated July 16, 1953—stopped working the claim, no vein."

"What did he mean by the sample number?" Karen asked.

"He kept all his ore samples in numbered boxes. They're on the bottom shelves. Help me look for the box labeled Wise River. It should be down here somewhere."

"I found it!" Andy exclaimed. "It's labeled Rain Gauge Mine, Wise River, Montana. It's heavy—somebody help me lift it up on the table."

Everyone bent over the box, lifting out the ore samples and reading the numbers either scratched into them, or tied around them with string.

"All the samples are here except for 37-42," Stephen remarked, as he placed the rock from Uncle Joe next to samples 30-35. "Look! They're the same. Joe's rock came from the same mine. Letty?" Stephen asked, as he suddenly turned toward her. "Letty, did you use samples 37-42 to fill in the spokes in the display at the Mining Museum?"

"My—that was 30 years ago—I don't know. Let me think. That was just when my Dad died. We needed some more rocks to finish out the wagon wheel. I believe I did use some rocks from one of these boxes, but I don't remember which one. That was a trying time for me. I vaguely remember wanting to find ore from the Orphan Girl, but Dad didn't have any left we liked from that mine. Maybe I took what I could find—I don't really know. I guess we figured no one would know where the rocks came from anyway."

"Letty, could you show us the mine, and could you loan us a shovel or two?" Stephen asked excitedly, as he headed for the door.

The mine was only a short drive from Letty's house. Since the 1950's trees and brush had grown over the site. Letty had enough shovels for the four of them to dig at once.

"Letty, I want to dig in the tailings," Stephen said. "Where should we dig?"

"What are tailings?" Andy asked, poking his shovel at several large rocks.

"They're diggings from the mine that are discarded since they don't contain any valuable ore."

"Why do we want to dig there if it's not valuable?"

"I want to see if we can find any rocks like Joe's and Letty's father's."

They started digging in the mound of dirt and rocks that Letty pointed out. With every shovelful they dug, several rocks similar to the numbered samples 30-35 appeared.

"This top layer must be the last they dug out of the mine," Stephen remarked. "Apparently they quit when all they could find was this same type of rock. I'll take a few with us for samples. Let's put the brush back over where we dug as best we can so it will look undisturbed. We've got to go back and see Martha. I want one last look at her scrapbook."

"Why, Dad?" Jill asked.

Stephen didn't answer. "Letty, if I find what I think I'll find, then it might be best to re-file a claim on this mine. Please don't tell anyone about our visit, or the mine. I'll call you from Martha's and let you know. Will it be possible to re-file?"

"It's possible, but who would want that pile of useless rock?" Letty asked.

"Who knows," was all Stephen said before they drove away. Back at Martha's house in Butte, Stephen bent over the picture of the wagon wheel. He adjusted the magnifying glass so he could clearly see the rocks in the spoke. Looking carefully, he could barely make out the scratched-in number. "38 WR," he read. "We'd better call Letty!"

CHAPTER TWENTY-TWO

STEPHEN

THEY SAT IN THE CAR at the top of Homestake Pass, elevation six thousand and some odd feet. Butte was only a few minutes west.

"Everyone out. We'll eat lunch at that picnic table where we can be easily seen from the road," Stephen said, reaching for the sandwiches they packed before leaving Butte. "I want anyone that's interested to see we're in no hurry, and that we're heading east."

"Dad, are we going to Glendive like you told the lady at the Mining Museum?" Andy asked.

"I'll tell you when we're eating. It'll give us something to pass the time since I want us to spend lots of time in view from the road."

Four sandwiches came out of the bag. Six eyes looked intently at Stephen. Each pair of eyes held steady as Stephen slowly unwrapped his sandwich, taking his time to lift up the top slice of bread and peer inside. Appearing satisfied at the way it looked, he took one careful bite. When he opened it back up to readjust the salami, they could take the waiting no longer.

"Dad!" Jill wailed.

"Stephen!" Karen demanded.

"You promised you'd tell!" Andy joined in.

"I did?" Stephen asked.

"Yes!!!!" all three voiced in unison.

"Well—if you're that anxious, and you can't wait until we get home, I guess I can tell you." Stephen took another bite of his sandwich, set it down and began. "Before we left on this trip I really didn't believe that Jim Fulton's and the car-jacker's disappearance had anything to do with any coded messages in the station reports. I didn't believe that the disappearances were anything more than that. Simply disappearances, that all. Besides, I didn't believe the scrambled station reports were really coded messages—there wasn't any concrete proof."

"But Dad, if you didn't believe it why did you ask us not to mention anything about Uncle Joe on our trip?" Jill asked.

"I wanted to add some fun to the trip by pretending I might actually believe in what Andy, Karen, and Gary were thinking. I thought a little mystery would make it more interesting. Besides, one thing was missing."

"Missing from our trip?" Jill wanted to know.

"No. Missing from their story. If some criminal organization would kill both Fulton and the car-jacker, and spend the money to set up a communications network that would reach worldwide, what's the motive?"

"Drugs?" ventured Karen.

"That's an easy answer, and we can add extortion, prostitution, smuggling, and so on. But those aren't really any better than listing baby-sitting. There are lots of reasons, but this whole thing—what can we call it?—suspected criminal activity—needs a definite motive to give it some glue, and to tie that motive to Butte and the Orphan Girl Mine to make it probable."

"And you have that motive?" Karen broke in.

"Maybe I do, and it could be nothing, but it could be everything. Remember that rock of Uncle Joe's?"

"Joseph Greeg said it was worthless," Andy responded. "It's full
of lutium—but no one wants lutium."

"It's lutetium, and don't be so sure. How would you like to have
your electricity bill cut to nothing? Electric cars that can run like
gas-powered ones? No more pollution? It's possible with superconductivity."

"Superconductivity?" Andy repeated.

"Wires that carry electricity without any resistance. A lot of
electrical energy goes into wasted heat. Whoever first develops
such a wire will make more money than all the drug dealers combined."

"I thought it was possible now," Karen added.

"Possible, but not practical. It's possible now only at extremely
low temperatures. About ten years ago, some ceramic metal oxide
compounds were found to be super-conductive at higher temperatures than previously known. These compounds contained some
rare earth elements. The temperatures weren't even close to room
temperatures, but the discovery fueled a race to try other combinations of rare earth elements with the idea of raising the
temperature to practical ranges. During the scramble to raise the
temperature, other combinations of elements were found to be as
good as rare earth elements. Since rare earth elements are expensive to obtain, that discovery essentially ended their use in
superconductivity. That is until now."

"What do you mean?" asked Karen.

"Well, as far as we know, no one has shown superconductivity
to be possible at even close to room temperatures. But suppose—
just suppose it is possible. Suppose that someone actually has discovered some combination of elements that works. And suppose

that combination of elements contains some rare earth element like lutetium, and that if a large supply of cheap lutetium was found it would be worth billions," Stephen said, holding up the sample of samarskite they got from Joe Macky. "Billions!"

"That's why the coded messages were about the Orphan Girl Mine," Jill blurted. "The Orphan Girl contains the lutetium!"

"Or so they think. No one, besides Martha, Letty, and ourselves, knows that the samples of samarskite didn't come from the Orphan Girl. The story about opening up the mine for tourists is just a cover. There are three main shafts and miles of tunnels off of each shaft. Some of the tunnels have probably collapsed. It could take months to check them all out. Months before they realize it's the wrong mine, and now we and Letty own the claim for the real source of the samarskite—the Rain Gauge Mine!"

"Then—that's why the samples of samarskite were removed from the spoke of the wagon wheel," Karen added.

"Yes, to hide them from anyone who might recognize them," Jill answered. "But why didn't they go to Letty, like we did, to ask about the samarskite?"

"I'm sure they didn't want to attract any attention to the samarskite. Besides, they had no reason to believe the samples weren't from the mine. They couldn't get the access to check out the mine without starting the tourist thing, and they couldn't get the permission to do the tourist thing if someone became too suspicious. What cinched it for me was when I discovered that the company that is opening the mine for tourists wanted the mineral rights before they'd start. Deep mining is too expensive today to make zinc, silver, or even gold valuable enough to mine from the Orphan Girl."

"But," Karen interjected, "not too expensive if the ore is worth billions."

"Do you think they discovered the superconductive wire, Dad?" Jill asked.

"I'm sure they didn't. They probably learned of it through industrial spying. Who knows how they learned about the Orphan Girl. It's all probable. If it's true, and they have already killed at least two people—then—then they won't hesitate to kill us as well. That's why I told the lady at the museum that we're heading east to Glendive to look for my uncle, but plan to stop along the way. That will give us several days' head start."

"Head start to get to Glendive?" Andy asked, looking around at the cars passing on the highway.

"We're not going to Glendive. We're going a few miles down the road, then turning off to an old hot springs. We'll wait there until after dark. Then we'll drive straight back home. But we won't actually go to our house. We'll stay in a motel under some made-up name. I need to talk to Gary about the code breaking. We may need more real proof before we go to Sergeant Grant, but we can't take any chances. If they are killers, they know how to do it without leaving any trace. We'd be gone and that would be it."

After dark, Karen and Stephen slipped away from Jill and Andy, and sat together looking at the lights dotting the valley below them.

"The stars," Karen began, "the stars are so bright and clear, I can see you as if the moon were out."

"It's a Montana night," Stephen answered. "It's Montana's way of saying come back—visit me again."

"I'd love to come back, but only with you and the kids. I wouldn't want to come without you. It just wouldn't be the same —" her voice trailed off.

"What's the matter?" Stephen asked her.

"I'm afraid."

"Of the killers?"

"No."

"Of what?"

"For us."

"For us?"

"I don't see how we can stay together, if you can't love me like a man should."

"I gave you the best sex you ever had."

"It's not enough. I need for you to hold me. I want to sleep in your arms at night. I want to have the same kind of sex, but with you—not by myself."

"Well, I've read that climaxes are stronger when people are by themselves, although they are more emotionally satisfying with someone else."

"I don't want to hear one of your logical explanations. I want you to tell me how you feel. Why is it you can't make love to me?"

"I can't tell you."

"If you can't tell me our relationship will die."

"You might die if I touch you."

"Are you sick?"

"Not with anything that can be cured."

"Is it AIDS?" Karen asked, a knot of fear swelling up in her stomach.

"It's nothing anyone can catch."

"Then how can touching me kill me?"

Stephen fell silent. Karen could hear his breathing above the muted noises of the night. It was slow and labored, like someone very old. Several times he stopped in mid-breath, as if he was going to speak, then he continued breathing without speaking.

"Stephen," Karen tried again. "If you're right about the Orphan Girl, we both might be dead soon. Please don't let me die not knowing why. I think I can stand never having you hold me, but I don't think I can stand not knowing why. You owe that much to me."

"Jill was just a little girl, and Andy had just been born. My wife was still in the hospital when they discovered a tumor. She couldn't stop bleeding after childbirth—we were both pretty scared."

"Janet didn't think you were ever married."

"No one knows outside of our family. We got married when she was nineteen and I was in graduate school. We met at the ocean. I never had any girlfriends up to then. I went camping with a friend on the beach. She came down with a group of young people from her church. I had made up my mind before I left that I was going to pick up a woman—actually for the first time in my life. The first time I met her, my friend took me aside and whispered in my ear, 'You're going to marry her.' I must have looked at him strangely, because he quickly added, 'She likes to joke around and you can take it.' He was right. We fell in love and were married. We started a family right away—she loved children —I sometimes pictured her as a grandmother—how happy I'd be in my old age having her for a partner—it was never to—to be."

"Oh, Stephen, I'm so sorry."

"I looked all around for treatments that might help. I found one on the east coast. It was experimental, but it really was her only hope. We left Jill and the baby with family, and flew there. I stayed with her the whole time—it was over in less than three weeks. The treatment was really hard on her. She just kept losing weight. Every day they would weigh her. We felt so bad when each time her weight dropped. We tried to keep our spirits up, but couldn't. The hospital let me sleep in the same bed with her. She became so weak that I had to carry her from the bed to the bathroom. Carrying her was like carrying a child. Towards the end, when I carried her, her legs and feet would hang down from under her nightgown. I'll never forget the way they looked. Have you seen the famous sculpture of Mary holding Jesus after he was brought down from the cross? Her feet looked just like Jesus' feet —the way they hung down, graceful and delicate. I thought of Jesus—how he died for others—I thought of her—how she gave her life to me and our children—how she was dying. I was lifting her from the bed to the bathroom when she asked me to hold her tighter. She was so frail that I was afraid I would hurt her—it didn't matter—she died in my arms. I stayed sitting on the bed rocking her gently in my arms. I brushed her hair back from her forehead and kissed it. I kept smoothing out the wrinkles in her nightgown. When the nurses discovered us, they finally lifted her out of my arms. She was so light that I didn't notice the weight was gone. I wanted to kill myself to end the pain. Every time I think about holding you—I—I picture her in my arms—how light she was—how even though I held her ever so tightly I couldn't hold her tight enough—I'm afraid you'll die if I hold you."

"I won't die."

"I'm afraid of going through that pain again."

"I won't make you."

"How can you not?"

"I'm younger than you and I'm healthy."

"I'm so afraid."

"Touch me, Stephen."

"Dad!" Andy yelled from the car. "It's plenty dark. I'm getting scared. Shouldn't we be going!"

Silently Stephen moved his partially outstretched hand away from Karen. "We're coming!" he yelled back, as they made their way back to the car. As he closed the door for Karen, she looked up at him and silently mouthed two words, "—Touch me."

CHAPTER TWENTY-THREE

FLOATING BRIDGE

"**D**AD? HOW COME we're staying next to the marina?" Andy asked, as Stephen unloaded suitcases from the trunk.

"It's close to the university. I've got to talk to Gary about the code-breaking program. This way he can walk down during lunch without arousing any suspicion—that is in case anyone is watching."

"Wow!" Jill exclaimed, as she opened the door to their room. "We never stay in any place this nice. Look, we have a view of the lake and the marina. If you stand right at the edge of the window you can just see the floating bridge. Andy! Dad? Does he have to open every drawer as soon as we get in a motel?"

"It's OK—it's just fun for him," Stephen replied. "Andy, maybe you could be a little quieter, and not rush around so much."

"Look, Dad!" Andy exclaimed. "The marina has power boats for rent. I always wanted to go out on a power boat. They open week-days at 6 in the morning. Can we rent one tomorrow—in the morning—before you see Gary?"

"Some day we can, but for now I don't want anyone to see us. When this whole mess is cleared up one way or another, then we'll come back."

"Phooey—I thought we could go and see if a pirate ship is really sunk in the channel."

"What channel?" Karen asked, joining the conversation.

"The channel that connects the Rushing River to the sound."

"The Rushing River?"

"Remember when you and Gary came out to our house? Dad's friend, old Professor Greenly left me his computer. Gary showed me how to run it. I figured out a pirate ship was deep in the channel. That's what's caused the currents to change. I'm sure of it!"

"Is that the channel where the drawbridge is?" Karen asked, trying to remember more about what Gary and Andy were doing.

"Yes—but who cares—now I'll never get to find the gold."

"You can't get to the channel from this lake anyway," Jill broke in, looking smug. "So it doesn't matter."

"Well, actually you can," Stephen countered. "It's a long way around, but it can be done. If you want to check out the channel, we can use Professor Greenly's boat. I don't think he'd mind. I'd like to hear how he's doing anyway. I'll call and ask him, but we can't do anything about any of this until we get everything else straightened out. Besides, we all need some sleep, and then maybe we won't be so much on edge. I just want to check to see if there are any messages on our phone at home."

Stephen dialed his home phone, punched in the code to trigger the replay mode, then set the motel phone to the conference speaker setting.

"Stephen, this is Janet. When you get back you need to call the chairman about the new students."

"Jill, can you call Louise at 432-8873?"

"This is Goodwill Industries. There will be a pickup in your neighborhood on September 18."

"Hi. This is Martha in Butte. Your friends did come by asking about you. They sure as anything made an odd couple. He's so slim, like a cowboy, and she's the exact opposite. Reminded me of the Lackmond boys—all tall and slim, like him—well, that's enough. You can call me if you want the details—bye."

They all looked at each other, but no one spoke.

"I doubt they're our friends," Stephen finally said.

"Do you remember what he told us at the $10,000 Silver Dollar Bar, about the Orphan Girl?" Jill asked. "He said it was a gold mine, but none of the samples in the wagon wheel from the mine were gold ore. How could he be a consultant if he didn't even know what kind of a mine it was?"

"I don't know what he is, but whatever it is, it's not good news for us," Stephen replied, his voice sounding grim. "This means they were tracking us from home. That's definitely not good. Not good at all. They probably think we're still heading to Glendive, but our time is probably short, no matter what they think now."

"Short?" Karen asked in a shaky voice.

"I don't mean short on this earth, I hope. Short—in terms of convincing the police that our lives are really in danger. If we don't have concrete proof to give them, nothing will come of it. Then if all this is true, they can kill us at their leisure without interference from the police. No. We have to have concrete proof, and only Gary can provide that. I'll call him right now. Everyone else—try to get some sleep. Don't go out. You can call for room service, but ask to have the food left outside the door."

"Where are you going, Dad?"

"To meet Gary, if he's home. I want to get started running the code-breaking program tonight. Now that we have an idea what might be going on, we can suggest words, like lutetium, for the program to try. Knowing some words to try could break the code in a day. Remember, don't go out, or let anyone in."

Karen fell into a heavy sleep, brought on by a combination of exhaustion and apprehension. Midway through the night she began to dream. Strange and disjointed dreams. Mine shafts that weren't really shafts, but tunnels into the Mining Museum. A museum that wasn't really a museum, but the drug garden at the university. The monkeys were laughing at her, but she couldn't hear what they were saying. Then she realized she was dreaming, and suddenly there was a way out of her regular dreams. She jumped up away from the ground, and flew into the night sky, up and away from the laughing monkeys.

Karen didn't care where she was flying, she was only glad it was away from her regular dreams. She flew over the university, then out over the dark lake towards the hills. Far below she noticed a light in a small house on the shore. Karen flew down to look in the window. Paintings lined the walls of the room in front—paintings of dead animals—disturbing paintings of people in the act of dying. Karen tried to pull away from the window, but one of the paintings began to shimmer. The colors were so vivid that she was drawn to the painting in spite of her fear. As she got closer, she noticed that her hands were shimmering like the painting. She stared at her hands, fascinated by the colors. Then she was plunged into darkness.

When her eyes adjusted to the dim light, Karen found she was in a damp underground room. Moonlight was coming through a small barred window high above her head. A chill cascaded through her as she began to make out piles of human bones stacked on stone shelves that lined the walls. She started to walk forward, but caught herself as fear overwhelmed her. There was another person standing in the shadows. A terrible taste filled her mouth as the moonlight illuminated long slender fingers thrusting towards her. The fingers began to explore the contours of her face, then settled on the curve of her neck.

"No, you didn't die from a broken neck," a man's voice came from out of the gloom. "How did you die? Come forward into the light so I can see you better."

Karen stood frozen, the long fingers slowly moving down over her shoulders.

"Did someone cut out your tongue? Let me see," he said, moving his fingers onto her lips. He stepped forword, into the moonlight. As he looked up at Karen, a shudder ran through her rigid body. It was the man at the marsh!

"Are you a spirit that has come to visit me? I want to know how you died. Was it a beautiful way? Tell me," he whispered as he pulled her into the moonlight.

Karen desperately wanted to end her lucid dream, but fear had immobilized her and she couldn't.

"Was it drowning? I love drowning. It leaves the body so intact —like yours," he continued, moving his hands slowly down her back and onto her waist. "Such lovely curves. Did you struggle when you died? What was it like to finally give yourself over when you stopped struggling? Did you enjoy it? I have a pet I feed, but when it eats its victims, they go into its watery stomach and drown. I'd like to know what it's like to drown. It's a pity I can't wait for you to tell me, but it's time to get my pet ready for feeding —such a pity—but I must go." He let his hand linger for a brief moment on her waist, then was gone. Karen fell toward the hard, cold stones of the floor, but just as she hit the stones they turned into sheets.

"Karen, you're shivering!" Jill exclaimed, as she drew back in alarm. "You smell musty, and your nightgown is damp—and your face—it's as white as the sheet. What happened?"

Karen wrapped the blankets around her cold body, trying to stop her shivering. "I had the worst dream ever. That man I had the nightmare about before in Montana—he--he--touched me with his long fingers. He thought I was dead. It was horrible! Stephen! I want to see Stephen."

"He's still gone with Gary," Jill replied, helping Karen draw the covers around her. "But, he'll be back later. He called while you were sleeping. He and Gary are leaving shortly to go out to our house."

"Your house?"

"Yes, Dad's friend at the Montana School of Mines left an electronic message on Dad's computer. He finished with the analysis of the sample. He sent it by overnight mail. Dad's afraid to leave it sitting in our box where anyone can read it so he and Gary are going to get it."

"Which way will they take to go home?" Karen asked, bolting upright in bed.

"Probably over the floating bridge. This time of the morning there isn't much traffic, so it's the quickest way."

"Will they have to go over the drawbridge?"

"It's the quickest way from the floating bridge," Jill replied, starting to become alarmed at Karen's questions. "Are they in danger?"

"Oh, Jill! Pray I'm not too late. Andy was right. The channel is blocked! How soon are they leaving?"

"Dad said they had an errand to run before they left. Is he going to die?"

"Not if I can help it. I'm going to stop him! As soon as I leave, call the police. Say you've just been assaulted by the tender at the Tidal Road Bridge, and are hiding from him in the bushes."

"In the bushes?"

"Say you're calling from a cellular phone, then scream or something—I don't know—make something up—only just do it!"

Before Karen slammed the door, she called back into the room, "And don't let anyone in, under any circumstances!"

Karen hurriedly crossed the parking lot, and ran down to the marina. "I need to rent a power boat, right now!" she yelled at the man under the sign that read 'Rent Boats Here.' "I'm in an awful rush. I have to meet someone across the lake in fifteen minutes and I overslept."

"I can have you out of here in ten minutes. I just need a major credit card. If you are willing to take the whole package including the extra insurance, that will speed things up since I won't have to explain everything."

"I'll take it. Just hurry. Where do I sign?"

"Please, God," Karen pleaded, as the boat sped away from the dock. "Don't let me be too late. I don't think I can live without him."

Karen steered the boat toward the middle of the floating bridge. When she came close enough to clearly see the passing motorists, she cut the engine and began to wave at the cars.

"Remember," she kept repeating to herself. "Remember how you liked to be naked in front of Stephen. How you enjoyed having him watch you. Just pretend this is one of your dreams and Stephen is standing on the bridge watching."

The rocking of the boat made it difficult for Karen to unbutton and remove her sweater, but when she waved it at the slowing cars, one or two began to stop. The morning sun felt warm on her breasts, as she braced herself with her legs to keep from falling over. She wondered if the people stopped on the bridge could see how much her legs were shaking. Some people had gotten out of their cars and were yelling something, but Karen couldn't hear them above the sound of the waves hitting the side of the bridge.

One person was taking pictures with a video camera. Karen reached down to unbutton her jeans, but was having trouble holding onto them: then she was momentarily distracted by the sound of an advancing helicopter. It was one of the morning traffic spotters. All at once the sky seemed filled with television helicopters hovering over her and small planes diving for a closer look. This added to the spectacle, and made the traffic jam worse that it had been. Karen had just gotten the top button of her jeans undone when a police launch pulled up beside her. The last thing Karen remembered before she hit her head was losing her balance as the wake from the launch caused her craft to pitch to the side.

CHAPTER TWENTY-FOUR

TOUCH ME

"YOU SAVED MY LIFE," Stephen said, walking down from where he was standing to sit beside Karen. They let their feet dangle in the pond, circles of water rippling away from them, each ripple a different color.

"How did you know what color I'd like the ripples?"

"If a man loves a woman, he should know what pleases her."

"Do you love me?"

"You know I do."

"When someone saves another's life, did you know that person belongs to the other from then on?"

"I might have heard that."

"Now that I own you, you must do what I ask. Is that clear?"

"Yes."

"I want you to love me like a normal man loves a woman. Do you understand what I'm asking of you?"

"Yes."

"Look at my breasts."

"They're beautiful."

"They saved your life."

"I know."

"You taught me to believe I'm attractive. Do you still believe that?"

"I love to look at your breasts."

"Would you like to touch them?"

"Very much."

"Well."

Stephen slowly reached out his hand toward her. Karen closed her eyes, leaned back on her arms, and held her breath.

EPILOGUE

WHEN DIVERS MADE a final count, they found six cars and eight bodies, including Fulton's and the car-jacker's, below the draw bridge. By the time the police had answered Jill's distress call, the bridge tender was gone. The company that intended to open the Orphan Girl Mine in Butte, Montana, withdrew from the project due to lack of funds. Gary couldn't break the code, but scrambled station reports stopped coming across the network. Stephen and Karen are still waiting for the announcement that room temperature superconductivity has been discovered.

Meanwhile, slender fingers traced the outline of the painting of the dying soldier. So sad, he thought with a sigh, it's hungry but I can't feed it anymore. Why won't they let me feed it anymore? I'll find new ways. They can't stop the creation of beauty. And death is so very beautiful.

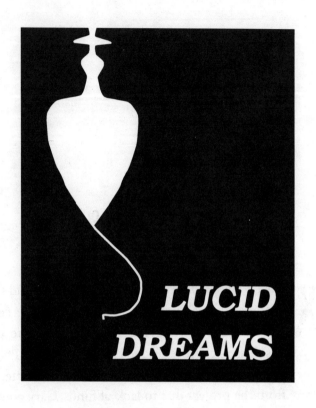

LUCID
DREAMS